Mary-Kate
and Ashley

mary-kate olsen   **ashley** olsen

so little time

Check out these other great
so little time
titles:

Book 1: **how to train a boy**

Book 2: **instant boyfriend**

Book 3: **too good to be true**

Book 4: **just between us**

Book 5: **tell me about it**

Book 6: **secret crush**

Book 7: **girl talk**

Book 8: **the love factor**

Book 9: **dating game**

Coming soon!

Book 11: **boy crazy**

mary-kate olsen   **ashley** olsen

so little time

a girl's guide to guys

by Nancy Butcher

Based on the teleplay by Becky Southwell

HarperEntertainment
An Imprint of HarperCollinsPublishers

A PARACHUTE PRESS BOOK

A PARACHUTE PRESS BOOK

Parachute Publishing, L.L.C.
156 Fifth Avenue, Suite 302
New York, NY 10010

Published by
HarperEntertainment

An *Imprint* of HarperCollins*Publishers*
10 East 53rd Street, New York, NY 10022-5299

Visit HarperEntertainment on the World Wide Web at
www.harpercollins.com

10 9 8 7 6 5 4 3 2 1

chapter
one

"**C**hloe!" fourteen-year-old Riley Carlson exclaimed to her twin sister. "It is *so* awesome to see you! What's new? How was your day? It's been so long. You have to tell me *everything*."

Chloe frowned at Riley. "Um, Riley? I just saw you at home. Like an hour ago."

Riley glanced around the women's rest room of their favorite café, the Newsstand. She peered under the doors of the stalls. The coast was clear—which was lucky, since the place was usually mobbed on Friday nights.

"Please don't make me go back out there," Riley whispered. "It's not safe."

"Why? What's going on?" Chloe narrowed her eyes at her sister. "Hey! Didn't you have a date tonight with Mr. Popularity?"

Riley nodded quickly. "Yes! And that's the whole

problem. He's out there right now. Waiting for me. I've been hiding in here for twenty minutes."

Chloe frowned. "Huh? Back up. I thought you liked him. What was it you said to me last night? 'If I'm out late with Todd, cover for me!'"

Riley winced. "Did I say that? I should have said, 'Help me run for cover!' He may be Mr. Popularity, but up close and personal, he's Mr. Shallow. If I have to talk to him for another minute, I'll die of boredom," Riley said. "I mean it."

"Wow, who would've guessed?" Chloe grinned and added, "Hey, if you die of boredom, then I'll be an only child. Can I have all your CDs and DVDs after you're gone?"

Riley punched Chloe's arm. This was *not* the time for humor. Didn't her sister realize that she, Riley, was having a dating emergency?

Ever since Riley and Vance had cooled things off, she'd been going out with other people. But she should have gotten to know Todd Granger better first. He was superpopular, but he was so into himself that she couldn't get a word in edgewise.

"I'm serious! I haven't been this bored since Mom and Dad made us watch that documentary about the history of cotton. Remember that one?" Riley complained.

Chloe nodded. "It was the best nap of my life."

Riley sighed. "All Todd does is talk about stuff I totally don't care about."

"Like what?" Chloe asked her.

Riley rolled her eyes. "Himself! You know, like this girl he dated last week and some other girl he dated the week before that. And he keeps trying to grab my hand, which I am *so* not into."

Chloe pulled a brush out of her backpack and ran it through her long wavy blond hair. "That *is* a problem. Look, I feel your pain. But you have to go back out there and face reality. Finish out the date. In thirty minutes tell him you have to go because, um, you have to get up superearly to visit our sick grandmother."

[**Riley:** **In case you were wondering, we don't have a sick grandmother. But Chloe is really good at coming up with stuff like that. It's probably because she was born eight minutes before me. She's got eight minutes more life experience than I do!]**

Riley considered her sister's advice. "Thirty minutes? I don't think I can last that long. Do you think *three* minutes will work?"

"How about fifteen?" Chloe suggested. "Three is way too short. There are rules about dumping a guy on the first date, you know?"

"I have a better idea," Riley said suddenly. "Let's switch outfits. You can go back out there and pretend to be me."

Chloe shook her head. "You've got to be kidding, right?"

"Come on, I'll pay you! I think I have six dollars in my wallet."

"Gosh, I am so tempted, but no, thanks," Chloe said. "Todd might wonder how your hair suddenly got so wavy. And how you grew a little taller. Besides, I'm hanging out with Amanda, Tara, and Quinn. And Lennon is working here later."

Riley noticed that Chloe's voice grew soft and dreamy when she mentioned Lennon's name. Lennon was Chloe's new guy. He was a major hottie, plus he was smart and sweet. And he seemed really crazy about her sister.

Riley also noticed that Chloe was wearing her best "I want to impress my new guy" outfit: red halter and killer denim skirt.

"Oh, all right," Riley said. "I guess I'll go back out there. It's the brave and honorable thing to do."

"Way to go," Chloe said with a grin. "You never know. Things could change. You might end up having an awesome evening."

"Or not," Riley said. "Bye, see you later." She checked her lip gloss in the mirror and headed out the door.

The Newsstand was packed with kids, many of them from West Malibu High, Riley and Chloe's school. Some of them were surfing the Internet on the café's computers.

Behind the counter, a girl with spiked blue hair was working the espresso machine. The air was filled with the delicious smells of coffee, cinnamon, and nutmeg.

Riley found Todd sitting at their table, sipping his decaf mocha. He smiled when he spotted Riley.

"I thought you fell in or something," he teased her.

Riley smiled tightly as she sat down in her chair. "No, no such luck."

"So, like I was saying," Todd said, leaning across the table, "we could check out that beach party later. This girl Randy is throwing it. You know her, right? She's the one who used to go out with Marcus, but then Marcus caught her in a major lip-lock with that Sanchez dude from the football team, so Marcus dumped her and now he's going out with Liza Jennings."

"Wow," Riley said, trying to sound enthusiastic. "I think Liza used to be in my French class. Hey, are you taking a language this year?" she said, changing the subject.

"Liza Jennings, *whoa*," Todd said as if he hadn't heard her question. "I wouldn't go out with her if you paid me. Word is, she dates every guy three times max and then dumps him with a nasty e-mail."

"Really?" Riley said. She checked her watch. What? Only two minutes? she said to herself.

She looked up at Todd. Speaking of time, it was time to try to change the subject again. "Sooooo. Have you heard the new Fang CD?"

Todd nodded quickly. "Yeah. It's kind of lame. They were playing it at this party I went to last Friday—hey, were you there? It was over at Erica Darrow's house. You know Erica, right? She's a junior, and she has her driver's license already, kind of, so that night she tried to borrow the keys to her dad's Jag...."

Riley glanced at her watch again.

[**Riley**: You're probably thinking—is this the same Riley Carlson we know and love? Sure, I'm into gossip just as much as the next girl, but not tonight. Is it Todd, or is it me? I mean, there's got to be more to life than talking about parties and old girlfriends. Well, at least for a little while, anyway.]

"I used to go out with Erica's sister Valerie. She's kind of cool, but she'll talk your ear off about modern dance and all that other weird artsy stuff she's into, which can get seriously tedious," Todd gabbed on. "I think I went out with Valerie's best friend, too. Susie something. I don't remember."

"That's nice," Riley said mechanically. She took a sip of her decaf cappuccino, which was cold now, and peeked at her watch. Twenty-six minutes to go! She was never going to make it.

Sighing, Riley glanced around. She spotted Chloe sitting at a table across the room with their friends Amanda Gray, Tara Jordan, and Quinn Reyes. The four of them were sharing a huge piece of carrot cake and cracking up about something. Riley sighed again. It looked like fun.

"Oh, great, they're, like, doing *folk* music now." Todd groaned.

Riley looked up. The espresso-machine girl with the spiked blue hair was standing on the stage. She tapped the microphone a couple of times. "Hello? Can everyone hear me?" she said.

"Yeahhhhh," the crowd droned in unison.

"I'm Cierra Frazier. That's Cierra with a C. I'm going to be reading some new poems tonight," the girl announced.

"Cool," Riley said. "And she almost has the same name as my friend, Sierra with an S."

"Poems?" Todd whispered to Riley. "Give me a break. Like we didn't get enough of that in Mr. Camino's class today!" Mr. Camino was their English teacher at West Malibu High.

Todd leaned over and grabbed Riley's hand. "Hey, let's get out of here. We could head over to that beach party."

Riley pulled her hand away and shook her head. "No, I want to stay."

And then a brilliant thought came to her.

Riley gave Todd a big smile. "But why don't *you* go ahead?" she suggested. "I wouldn't want you to miss out on *the* party of the weekend!"

Please-say-yes-please-say-yes-please-say-yes, she chanted to herself.

"Without you? No way," Todd said.

Rats! Riley thought. She checked her watch again. Twenty-three minutes to go.

Cierra tapped on the mike again. She pulled a crumpled-up piece of purple paper out of her jeans pocket. She smoothed it out, and then she began to read:

"I wish I could cry about you,
But instead I do my nails
And read magazines I've read a hundred times before.
I wish I could cry about you,
But instead I talk to my cat
And…"

"She talks to her *cat*?" Todd said, rolling his eyes.

Riley glared at him. "Shh! I'm trying to listen," she whispered.

Todd made a face. "Why?"

"Don't you get it?" Riley whispered. "She can't deal with her pain, so she numbs it out by reading the same magazines over and over again. And she talks to her cat. Stuff that's kind of mindless, but at least it takes her mind off her heartache." She sighed. "It's such a simple poem, but it's so raw. So honest."

Todd stared at her. "Okay, whatever."

Cierra finished that poem and began another one—this time about broken friendships. Riley had to admit, she really liked Cierra's poems. She had always thought that poems were old and dusty and boring. But Cierra's poems were so passionate.

When Cierra finished the last poem, a few people

clapped politely. One of the guys behind the counter cranked up the CD player, and a loud Weevils song began blasting on the speakers.

"Okay, that's our cue to go." Todd stood up and grabbed Riley's hand. "Come on, babe, it's beach-party time!"

Riley checked her watch. *Yes! Thirty minutes!*

She yanked her hand back. "Um, you know, I have this massive headache. And my grandmother is sick. I should really be heading back." She got up from her chair.

"What's the deal with your grandmother?" Todd asked. "What's wrong with her?"

"A massive headache. Same thing! It runs in the family," Riley blurted out. "Anyway, I'll just go home."

"I'll walk out with you," Todd offered.

Riley grabbed her purse and headed out the exit, followed by Todd. Outside, the evening sea breeze was warm and salty. Freedom! Fresh air! Riley turned to Todd to say a final good night.

But before she could say the words, she saw his lips heading in the direction of her lips.

[Riley: No, it couldn't be...yes, it could...he's going to...oh, gross!]

She felt Todd's hands snake around her shoulders. She felt his hot breath against her face. He smelled like hot chocolate and garlic.

Defensive action, Riley told herself the mere micro-second before Todd's kiss-motion was complete. She spun her head quickly to the left. Todd's lips landed on her right cheek.

"Good night! Had a great time!" Riley said with a wave. Before Todd had a chance to say anything, Riley raced off down the sidewalk.

Thank goodness that's over, Riley thought, wiping her wet cheek. Now I won't have to deal with Todd ever again!

chapter two

Chloe swirled her spoon through her iced latte. Tara was telling her, Quinn, and Amanda about her new laptop computer. But Chloe could barely concentrate on Tara's words. All she could think about was Lennon, Lennon, Lennon.

[Chloe: You're probably wondering who Lennon is. Lennon Porter is the perfect guy. He's smart, he's sweet, and he's supercute. And the best part is, he's my boyfriend.]

"Um, Earth to Chloe!" Tara said. She waved her hands in front of Chloe's eyes. "Hello? Are you there or what?"

"I'm here!" Chloe said. "You were just talking about…modems?"

Tara giggled. "That was, like, half an hour ago. Now we've moved on to our favorite DVDs."

"I think someone's in looooove," Quinn said to Tara, her eyes twinkling.

Chloe felt her cheeks turning red. "I am not!" she insisted. "I'm just in…major *like*."

"Chloe's in love, Chloe's in love," Tara chanted. Quinn and Amanda joined in.

Chloe spotted Lennon coming through the front door. She kicked at Tara, Quinn, and Amanda under the table. "Shh!" she hissed.

At the sight of Lennon's dreamy face and his wind-tousled hair, Chloe felt her heart do a somersault. No, more like a triple axel on skates. He looked really hot in his jeans and baggy faded indigo T-shirt.

Lennon headed over to their table. His eyes locked with Chloe's, and he gave her a happy, lopsided smile. "Hey, Chloe," he called out. "Hey, guys," he said to the other three girls.

"Hey, Lennon," Chloe replied. She touched his arm. "How's it going? I've missed you!"

Lennon nodded. "I had to get a head start on my biology paper. It's due Monday. Hey, you look cute today. Cool outfit."

Chloe melted. "Thanks! Really? That was so nice." She looked at her friends. "Wasn't that nice, guys?"

"Definitely nice, Chloe," Amanda said.

"You look great today, too, Lennon," Chloe said, smiling. "I love that casual look you've got going on. And how do you get your hair into such perfect spikes?" she asked. She thought she heard Tara groan, but she wasn't sure.

Lennon blushed. "It's that hair gel that comes in a purple tube. Hey, I think my shift's about to start." He nodded toward the counter.

"I'll see you later, okay?" Chloe leaned forward and gave him an even bigger smile.

"Sounds good to me. Maybe we can split a white mocha hot chocolate," Lennon suggested.

He leaned over and kissed her on the cheek. His lips were so soft and warm. Chloe tried not to swoon. She wasn't sure what that word meant exactly—*swoon*—but that's how she felt right now.

Lennon waved at the girls and took off toward the espresso bar.

Chloe turned to Tara, Quinn, and Amanda. "Oh, isn't he the best?" she gushed. "I am so lucky to be going out with him. He is so perfect, and our relationship is…so perfect!"

Quinn gave her a funny look.

Chloe clamped her hand over her mouth. "Oh, I shouldn't say stuff like that, should I?" she mumbled. "I might jinx it. I don't want to mess it up. I haven't exactly had great luck with guys lately."

[Chloe: Yeah. Let's just say my last boyfriend paid more attention to his dirt bike than he did to me. And he turned out to be a real creep. Well, I hope he and his bike are happy together.]

Quinn and Tara exchanged a glance. Then they both stared at Chloe as if she were an alien from outer space.

"What?" Chloe demanded. "Did I just sprout a giant zit on my nose?"

"Oh, it's nothing," Tara said finally.

Chloe knew better than to believe that. "It is *not* nothing. Tell me what it is!" she insisted.

Quinn dipped her finger into the frosting of the carrot cake they were all sharing and licked it off. "Well—I just hope you don't lose Lennon," she began.

"What?" Chloe and Amanda said in unison.

"You're kind of going about this thing with Lennon all wrong," Quinn explained.

Chloe gasped. "What is it? Do I have bad breath? Do I have lip gloss on my teeth?" She began rummaging through her purse for a mirror.

Tara shook her head. "No, it's not like that. The thing is, you're way too…I don't know…gushy with him."

Chloe's eyes grew huge. "What do you mean?"

"'How do you get your hair into such perfect spikes?'" Quinn repeated, imitating Chloe's voice.

"I didn't sound like that!" Chloe protested. "Did I?"

"Chloe was just being nice," Amanda said.

Chloe nodded. "Yeah. I mean, Lennon is so awesome. He's the most awesome guy I've ever known. We talk on the phone six times a day. We send each other silly e-mails all the time. He knows all my favorite songs, and I know his, and…and…"

Quinn slapped her hand on the table. "See? You're proving our point. You're being gushy again!"

"If you want to keep a guy interested, you have to act way cooler than you're acting," Tara added.

Amanda made a face. "Cooler? What's that supposed to mean?" she asked Tara.

"Chloe shouldn't act like she's so…so *into* Lennon," Tara explained. "She should act like she could take him or leave him."

"But I don't *want* to leave him!" Chloe said.

Quinn slapped the table with her hand again. "Exactly! That's why you have to act like you *could* leave him," she said firmly.

Chloe considered it. She knew that Tara and Quinn were two of her coolest friends. They were always wearing the hottest clothing trends before anybody else. And they were way into giving advice. Good advice.

Maybe I should hear them out, Chloe thought. "I see your point—sort of." She frowned. "But how can I stop being gushy with him? It just comes out of my mouth."

"We are so glad you asked," Tara said with a big grin. "Quinn and I found the most awesome Website. It'll tell you everything you need to know."

Quinn flipped her hair over her shoulders. "Yes, Tara, that's excellent! Chloe should be following the Guide!"

"*What* guide?" Chloe and Amanda said in unison.

Tara grinned. "Follow the master. Listen and learn."

Tara got up from her chair and headed over to one of the computer stations. Quinn, Chloe, and Amanda trailed after her. Tara punched some keys to get onto the Internet.

After a minute Tara was on a teen dating Website. It had an image of a girl and a guy staring dreamily at each other over pizza and candlelight.

On the corner of the page was a menu. Tara hit the link that said the Guide.

After a moment a new page popped up on the screen. Chloe leaned forward. She was really curious about this guide thing, whatever it was. She read the notes on the screen:

**A GIRL'S GUIDE
TO GETTING AND KEEPING GUYS**

1. **If you want to meet a guy you're interested in, walk by him slowly and totally ignore him at the same time.**
2. **Once you're dating a guy, don't gush or otherwise show him how you feel about him.**
3. **Don't accept a date with less than three days' notice.**
4. **The second time he asks you out for a Saturday night, tell him you're busy.**
5. **Never call him first, unless it's to cancel a date.**

6. **Wait at least six hours before returning his calls or e-mails.**

7. **Don't kiss him until the fourth date—at least.**

8. **Make sure he sees you hanging out with friends and busy with other activities. Make him think you're in demand.**

9. **If he compliments you on your jewelry, be vague about where you got it. Let him think it's from an old boyfriend.**

10. **If you see him hanging out with another girl, don't ask him who she is or act as if you care. Act superconfident and secure!**

Tara scrolled down the page. There was more.

I had the worst luck with guys—until I tried the Guide! Now my phone never stops ringing!
—Marya, La Jolla

This guy didn't know I existed until I tried the Guide. Within three days he was a total love puppy. Thank you, Guide!
—Sarabeth, Boulder

I was dating this guy I really liked. I didn't want to lose him, so I put the Guide into action. It worked like magic, and now we've been a major item for six whole months. Guide, I owe it all to you!
—Kelly, Fort Lauderdale

There were dozens more stories like that. Tara jabbed her finger at the screen. "See? It works!"

Chloe reached over to the keyboard and scrolled up to the ten rules again. She read them a second time.

"I don't know," Chloe said slowly.

Amanda shook her head. "Some of these rules seem kind of weird. Like this one: 'Wait at least six hours before returning his calls or e-mails.' I mean, how cruel is that?"

"Plus, some of the rules seem totally impossible," Chloe added. She was thinking about rule number seven, although she didn't say so out loud. Even though she and Lennon hadn't kissed yet, she could hardly wait. They'd been on only one official date. How was she supposed to hang on until their fourth?

Also, if she ever saw him hanging out with another girl, there was no way she was going to act superconfident and secure. She would rather dump a strawberry smoothie all over his head!

"These rules are hard work, but they're worth it!" Tara said, interrupting Chloe's thoughts. "You read what Kelly in Fort Lauderdale said. Kelly is just like *you*, Chloe! If the Guide worked for her, it'll definitely work for you, too."

"I don't know, guys," Amanda said doubtfully. "Things are really cool between Lennon and Chloe right now. Why should she act differently?"

"Things are going really well *now*," Quinn pointed

out. "The Guide is about making sure it *stays* that way. I know this girl in L.A. who liked this guy. But she couldn't get past the 'just friends' stage with him. Then she tried the Guide, and everything changed. They've been together for three months!"

"Really?" Chloe said, impressed.

Quinn nodded.

"The Guide is the way to go," Tara chimed in.

Chloe looked across the room at Lennon. He was making cappuccinos. He caught her eye and smiled at her. She smiled back but inside she felt uncertain.

What if Quinn and Tara were right? Maybe she *was* too gushy and eager with Lennon. Maybe she *could* stand to wait more than thirty seconds before returning his e-mails. Kelly and the other girls who'd posted their stories on the teen Website seemed pretty happy with their relationships—thanks to the Guide.

"Okay, I'll try it," Chloe said finally.

Tara and Quinn exchanged high fives.

"Yes!" Tara said.

"Trust me," Quinn added, "you'll be glad you did this."

Chloe laughed. "Maybe you're right."

"No," Amanda said, "you're all wrong. These rules are silly. They'll never work."

"But they worked for Kelly from Fort Lauderdale and Sarabeth from Boulder and Marya from La Jolla, and Tara's friend from L.A.," Chloe pointed out.

"And that's called proof!" Tara said.

"Yeah, if you think the Guide doesn't work, then maybe *you* should prove it," Quinn told Amanda.

Amanda grinned. "Fine! I will!"

Chloe wasn't sure Amanda could do it. The Guide had already worked for tons of girls. But Chloe couldn't think about Amanda right now. She had to start studying the Guide right this second!

chapter three

On Monday morning Riley doodled in her notebook as Mr. Camino, her English teacher, talked about English Romanticism. She was trying to avoid Todd, who kept smiling at her from across the room.

Some people never get the hint, Riley thought. Maybe I need to write him a Dear Todd letter. She scribbled it out next to a doodle of a butterfly:

Dear Todd,
Give it up.
            Sincerely,
            Riley Carlson

She scratched it out and started another one.

Dear Todd,

"Can anyone tell me what Keats, Byron, and the other English Romantic poets had in common?" Mr. Camino asked the class.

Larry Slotnick, Riley and Chloe's next-door neighbor, raised his hand. Larry was nice but he was kind of on the goofy side.

[**Riley**: **And maybe I should tell you that Larry's had a crush on me since first grade. For a while I thought he was over it because he started dating my best friend, Sierra. But then they broke up. Sierra said he wouldn't stop talking about me. Luckily, Sierra didn't seem too bummed about the breakup, or we could have had a best-friend problem.**]

Mr. Camino pointed to Larry. "Yes, Larry?"

"They bought lots of flowers and CDs for their girlfriends?" Larry guessed.

Mr. Camino frowned. "Uh, no, Larry. They wrote about the inevitability of loss and change. For example, they might write about how beautiful a summer day was...but how it would soon be gone and turn into autumn and winter."

"What's the problem with that? That's football and basketball season," Todd spoke up.

"Yes, well, that's not how Keats and Byron and their colleagues saw it," Mr. Camino replied. He picked up a small book with a cracked leather binding. "I'm going to read you all something by Byron. Notice the themes of loss and change."

Mr. Camino gave a small cough, then began to read:

"'When we two parted
In silence and tears,
Half broken-hearted
To sever for years,

Pale grew thy cheek and cold,
Colder thy kiss;
Truly that hour foretold
Sorrow to this.

The dew of the morning
Sunk chill on my brow—
It felt like the warning
Of what I feel now....'"

Riley stopped doodling and listened to the Byron poem. It was so honest and beautiful, like a really cool love song. It reminded her of the poems Cierra Frazier had read last Friday at the Newsstand—only the language Byron used was more formal.

She would have to e-mail Sierra and tell her about Cierra Frazier and Byron.

Sierra was a musician, so she'd appreciate poetry, which was kind of like song lyrics. Sierra was out of school with a nasty case of the flu. Riley missed having her around.

After Mr. Camino had finished reading the poem, he said, "Can anyone tell me what that was about?" He scanned the class.

Riley raised her hand.

"Yes, Riley?" Mr. Carlson pointed to her.

"This guy—I'm guessing it was a guy—broke up with someone years ago," Riley explained. "He felt really bad then because she was so cold to him. But it's not nearly as bad as how he feels now, because he really misses her."

Mr. Camino beamed. "Exactly. Very good, Riley." He turned to the rest of the class. "Now that you have a sense of what a good poem is all about, I'd like you to try a hand at writing your own."

"This assignment is going to help me get into law school *how*?" a girl named Lauren spoke up.

"Why don't you write a poem about the Constitution?" Mr. Camino suggested, raising his eyebrows. He turned to the rest of the class. "You can choose any topic you'd like and any of the forms we've studied— sonnet, free verse, blank verse. They will be due by Friday."

A chorus of groans rose in the air. But Riley was smiling. She couldn't wait to try her hand at composing a poem. She picked up her pen and wrote on her doodle sheet, next to a picture of a surfboard:

Poem for Eng. Class by Fri.!!!

The bell rang. "Tomorrow we'll be talking about the poets Ezra Pound and T. S. Eliot," Mr. Camino called out as the students stood and shuffled out of the classroom.

Riley grabbed her backpack and books and headed for the door. Just before she got out to the hall, she felt a hand on her shoulder.

She turned around. It was Todd.

Uh-oh, she thought.

Todd flashed her a toothy grin. "Hi, gorgeous. So, tell me. What's up?"

"Uh, hi, Todd," Riley replied.

Todd looked her up and down, checking out her new skirt and beaded top. "You look really hot in that outfit," he complimented her. "Hey, how's your headache? How's your sick grandmother? Do you want to go out again Friday night?"

Riley thought quickly. "Fine, fine, and no, I don't think so. But thanks for asking, anyway!"

Riley waved good-bye before Todd had time to make her another offer. She made a beeline for the study hall room, found an empty table, and sat down quickly.

Riley glanced up to see if Todd had followed her, but there was no sign of him.

[Riley: You'd think that guys would get it. You know, if she smiles, flips her hair, and thinks the

spinach in between your teeth is cute, it means
she's interested. If she makes a lame excuse to
cut the first date short, it means she's not.]

The bell rang. Riley pulled a notebook and pen out
of her backpack. Then she settled back and tried to think
of some ideas for her poetry assignment.

Let's see…what should I write about? Riley asked
herself. My favorite CD? Jewelry? The beach? Yes, the
beach!

She picked up her pen and began writing:

I love the beach.
It's such a…

What rhymes with beach? Riley wondered. She
scratched out the last line and wrote:

It is better than eating a peach.
I love surfing at high tide.
It's such an awesome ride.
I love looking for shells

Riley paused. What rhymed with *shells*? *Bells*, *swells*,
tells. But none of those words really fit.

She read over what she had written so far. It wasn't
as good as Cierra's poems, and it definitely wasn't as
good as Byron's.

And I don't even *like* peaches, Riley told herself. She

crossed out the entire poem and turned to a clean page. Now what? she wondered.

"Excuse me," a boy said.

Riley glanced up. A guy from her algebra glass was standing next to her. Malcolm Golden. He was super-cute, with curly brown hair and dark brown eyes.

"Hey, Malcolm," she said.

"Hey, Riley," Malcolm said. "Listen, I was wondering...do you want to go out with me sometime?"

[Riley: Whoa! I know at least ten girls who'd kill to go out with Malcolm Golden.]

"Um, sure," Riley said, smiling up at him.

"How about later today? Are you free?" Malcolm asked her.

Riley nodded. "Yeah. I was going to go to the beach, but we could hang out instead."

"Great," Malcolm said. "I'll come by your locker after eighth period."

After Malcolm went back to his table, Riley couldn't stop smiling. From Todd Granger to Malcolm Golden. How awesome was that?

"Hey, Riley."

Riley glanced up again. Dan, a guy from her English class, was standing there, sipping a soda.

"I was wondering if you were busy Saturday night," Dan said. His blue eyes twinkled as he smiled.

Riley couldn't believe it. I'd better look up my love

horoscope on the Web, she thought. This must be my lucky day!

It was Monday afternoon—two more classes to go. Chloe reached into her locker and pulled out a couple of textbooks.

"I checked out the Guide Website again over the weekend," she said to Amanda, Tara, and Quinn, who were waiting to walk down the hall with her. "I can't wait to try out the rules on Lennon."

"I still think you're making a mistake," Amanda told her, brushing a strand of hair out of her eyes.

"How can you say that after Friday night?" Tara asked Amanda.

Amanda frowned. "Huh? What happened Friday night?"

"Chloe's own *sister* used the rules," Quinn explained. "On Todd. They had a hot date, and now she's acting as if she doesn't like him."

"She *doesn't* like him," Chloe pointed out.

Tara smiled. "That's not what Todd is saying. He said that they made out on the beach. And now Riley is ignoring him. It's all over school."

Chloe gasped. "What? That totally did *not* happen! What do you mean it's all over—"

Just then a girl with short blond hair came rushing out of the girls' bathroom. Her eyes were red, and she had black mascara blotches on her cheeks.

Chloe stopped talking and stared after the girl. She'd obviously been crying.

Quinn sighed. "Poor Adrienne," she whispered. "It's so sad."

"Why? What's wrong with her?" Chloe whispered back. "Why is she crying?"

"She met Peter Millis by using the Guide," Tara explained in a low voice. "They were a hot item for a while. Then she stopped following the rules. And guess what? He broke up with her this weekend—by *e-mail*. Can you believe it?"

Amanda looked doubtful. "That's not what I heard. I heard that Peter just started liking someone else."

"Well, we all know *why*," Quinn said. "Five letters. G-U-I-D-E. Need I say more?"

"Wow, the rules in the Guide are really powerful," Chloe said.

Amanda rolled her eyes. "I am so sick of hearing about the Guide! It's so stupid."

"Hey, didn't you say you were going to prove the Guide doesn't work?" Tara asked Amanda. "When is that going to happen?"

"Well, Amanda?" Quinn added.

Amanda nodded. "I'll do it. I thought of a plan over the weekend. I'm going to use the rules on some guy I don't know, and he won't even notice that I'm alive. That'll prove once and for all that the rules don't work." She looked up and down the hall nervously. "I—I just have to find a candidate for my little experiment."

Chloe scanned the hall, too. She knew Amanda was shy and would have a hard time getting her experiment going. Then Chloe spotted *the* guy.

"There he is," she said, pointing to a boy who was searching for something in a locker across the hall. "Bobby Flynn!"

"Bobby Flynn? Are you crazy, girl?" Tara asked, shaking her head.

Bobby Flynn was cute, with curly blond hair and blue eyes. So far he hadn't given Amanda—or any of them, for that matter—the time of day.

"Perfect!" Quinn giggled. "Go for it, Amanda. Try rule number one. 'If you want to meet a guy you're interested in, walk by him slowly and totally ignore him at the same time,'" she recited.

"Wow, you have the rules memorized," Chloe said, impressed.

Amanda glanced at Bobby shyly. Chloe could tell that she wasn't sure about going through with this.

"You can do it," Chloe encouraged her.

Amanda smiled anxiously. "I guess. Okay, here I go. But I'm telling you, I can do rule one for days and Bobby isn't going to notice me."

Chloe, Quinn, and Tara stared, mesmerized, as Amanda headed down the hall in Bobby's direction. Just as she was about to pass him, he closed his locker and turned around.

Amanda slowed down—just like the rule said to do—and.didn't look at Bobby once.

But Bobby looked at *Amanda*. And looked. And looked.

He couldn't seem to take his eyes off her.

Amanda circled back around to the girls. "See?" she started to say. "The rules don't—"

"Hey, Amanda?"

Chloe turned her head and saw Bobby rushing down the hall toward them.

"Oh, wow," Tara whispered, elbowing Chloe.

"Hey," Bobby said breathlessly, as he stopped in front of Amanda. "Could I talk to you alone for a second? I'm Bobby Flynn. I was wondering if you were doing anything tonight—"

Chloe gasped. She had just seen it with her own eyes. There was no doubt about it. *The Girl's Guide to Getting and Keeping Guys* really worked!

chapter four

Riley had once heard her dad use the expression "Rainy days and Mondays always get me down." It was a line from an old cheesy song from the 1970s that he liked. He always said Mondays were sad because he had to go to work and his job had a lot of pressure.

[**Riley**: But that was when Dad was working. You see, he and my mom were both high-powered fashion designers. They were even partners. Then Dad got burned out on the whole executive thing and decided to take a break from the pressure for a while. Now he lives in a trailer and reads a lot of books on finding your Inner Self. Mom is still a high-powered everything.]

But Riley had had a totally awesome Monday. She was on a great date with Malcolm, whom she'd never even had a conversation with before. He was fun and interesting. He liked the beach and old movies, just like she did. And on top of that, three more guys had asked her out that afternoon at school. First there was Dan. Then Connor. Then Angel.

[Riley: **It's like a world record for me to get asked out four times in one day—even four times in one week or one month. Maybe it's my new perfume or something. Ha-ha.**]

After school Riley and Malcolm went Rollerblading on the boardwalk. Then they picked up some iced cappuccinos at the Newsstand.

Now they were walking back to her house. Riley was glad that she was carrying her Rollerblades in one hand and her cappuccino in the other. Otherwise, Malcolm might try to hold her hand. And she wasn't sure she was ready for that. Maybe on their second date.

Soon they were at her house, which was right on the beach. Through the living room window Riley could see the family housekeeper, Manuelo, cleaning the furniture with a big feather duster.

Riley stopped at the front door. She turned and smiled at Malcolm. "Thanks, I had an awesome time. I'll see you at school tomorrow, okay?"

"Definitely," Malcolm said. He set his Rollerblades down on the ground. Then all of a sudden he grabbed Riley around the waist. He leaned forward to kiss her.

Huh? Riley thought, wriggling away. "Okay, well,

good-bye. I have to be going now," she said quickly.

But Malcolm didn't seem to get the hint. He pulled her toward him and tilted his head and leaned in again.

Riley pulled away again. She was starting to get mad. "Um, Malcolm? I usually don't kiss on the first date," she explained, trying to keep her voice even.

Malcolm gave her a strange smile. "That's not what I heard."

Uh-oh, I don't like the sound of this, Riley thought. "What are you talking about?" she demanded.

"I heard you're a great kisser," Malcolm added.

Riley felt her cheeks flush with heat. "Where did you hear that?"

"Oh, come on. *Everyone* knows about your date with Todd last Friday," Malcolm said with a grin.

> [Riley: I'd better count to ten or hold my breath or something. Because if I don't, I'm going to start screaming. Todd! He's been spreading lies around the whole school!]

"That *toad*," Riley muttered under her breath.

"What did you say?" Malcolm asked her.

Riley shook her head. "Nothing. I have to go kill Todd now. I mean, I have to go."

Malcolm picked up his Rollerblades. "Sure. You want to do this again tomorrow night? Maybe then you'll kiss me like you kissed Todd."

Or not! Riley thought. She glared at Malcolm. "That

would be great, but I'm busy. I'm busy Wednesday, too, and Thursday and Friday. And every other night for the rest of my life. Bye, now!" She stormed inside the house and slammed the door behind her.

Inside, she took a deep breath, and then another. Part of her wanted to cry. The other part wanted to strangle Todd. So that's why all those boys had asked her out— because of some stupid rumor Todd had started!

She took off her backpack and resisted the temptation to throw it across the room. Wait until she got her hands on that *toad!*

Chloe leaned against a palm tree and glanced at her watch. Lennon was supposed to meet her at the beach fifteen minutes ago. They had a date to go for a walk and then to study at her house.

"He definitely said Monday after school," Chloe muttered to herself. "Where *is* he? He wasn't late for our *first* date. He was fifteen minutes early!"

> [Chloe: You don't think he's already losing interest in me, do you? Maybe I should have been using the rules in the Guide from the very beginning—like, our first date. Oh, no, what if it's too late?]

Just then Lennon came running down the sidewalk. Chloe's anxieties totally vanished at the sight of his adorable face. He hadn't lost interest in her. She felt silly for thinking that—even if it was for only a minute.

"Hey," Chloe called out with a smile.

"Hi," Lennon said as he stopped in front of her. He squeezed her arm and kissed her cheek. "I'm sorry I'm late. I kind of had this emergency."

Chloe frowned. "You had an emergency? What kind of emergency?"

Lennon sighed. "You know that history quiz I got back from Ms. Simmons today? I didn't do too well on it. She's giving me a chance to take it over. But I have to do it right now."

Chloe's heart sank. "R-right now?" she murmured.

Lennon nodded. "I'm really sorry. I promise I'll make it up to you."

Chloe had never heard of Ms. Simmons letting anybody take a quiz over again. Still, she wasn't going to question Lennon about it. Be sympathetic, Chloe told herself.

"No problem," she said, forcing herself to sound cheerful. "Good luck with the quiz! Call me later and tell me how you did."

Lennon smiled. "Definitely. I'll talk to you later!"

He took off across the school parking lot. Chloe felt her heart sinking even more. She had really been looking forward to spending some time with him.

As soon as she got home, Chloe grabbed a snack, shut herself in her room, flopped onto her bed, and called Quinn on her cell phone. "Quinn? Where are you?" Chloe demanded as soon as Quinn picked up.

"Tara and I are at the mall. Where are you? I thought you had a date with Mr. Perfect," Quinn replied.

Chloe told Quinn about Lennon's history-quiz emergency.

"Yeah, right. History-quiz emergency my foot," Quinn said after she'd finished. "That is the *lamest* excuse I've ever heard! Girl, I'm telling you. He's starting to lose interest."

"Give me that phone, Quinn!" Chloe heard Tara demand.

"Chloe, you have to activate the rules right now," Tara ordered her.

"I know, I totally agree," Chloe said. "I'm going to go on-line and print them out right now."

Quinn grabbed the phone back from Tara. "Remember, play hard to get! Pretend that he's the hunter and you're the bunny! You have to hop, hop, hop on your little bunny legs to get away! Run, bunny, run!"

Hunters? Bunnies? "Quinn, you're scaring me," Chloe told her.

After she said good-bye to Tara and Quinn, Chloe logged on to her computer. She typed in the address for the Guide Website and printed out the page of rules. She placed the printout on her desk, next to her computer.

Then Chloe's computer made a jingling noise. Someone was trying to instant-message her.

A box popped up onto the screen:

LENNON256: Would like to send you a
message. Do you want to accept it?

Chloe's heart skipped a beat. Then she reminded
herself what Quinn had said: Hop like a bunny. Don't be
too eager. She counted to ten, and then she typed *yes*.
A second later, Lennon wrote back:

LENNON256: Hey, Chloe. I just finished
the quiz. I'm still at school.

CHLOE494: How did it go?

LENNON256: I think I did okay. Listen,
I'm sorry about canceling today.

Chloe wasn't sure whether to believe his excuse or
to listen to Quinn and Tara. But she did know what the
Guide would say. Act like it's no big deal!

CHLOE494: Don't worry about it.

LENNON256: There's going to be a meteor
shower tonight. Are you interested? We
could meet on the beach.

Chloe was about to type YES!!!! But then she
remembered to check the Guide first.

She glanced at the printout. There it was:

3. Don't accept a date with less than three days' notice.

Chloe nodded, determined. As much as she wanted to see Lennon, she had to follow each and every rule. She typed:

```
CHLOE494: I have plans tonight. Many,
many plans.

LENNON256: How about tomorrow or Wed.?
We could do something else.
```

Chloe felt a wave of excitement. She had just started using the Guide on Lennon and he was already begging to go out with her. She wrote back:

```
CHLOE494: Plans then, too. Sorry.

LENNON256: Thursday?
```

Chloe counted on her fingers: Tuesday, one. Wednesday, two. Thursday, three. Three days! Thursday would not be against the rules.

But don't sound too eager, she reminded herself. Be the bunny. Hop. Whatever.

```
CHLOE494: Sure, I guess.

LENNON256: Great! Can I call you later?

CHLOE494: I may be out, but you can
try.

LENNON256: I'll see you at school
tomorrow, then. I can't wait. I really
miss you.
```

Lennon misses me! Yes! Chloe thought, pumping her fist in the air. The Guide is incredible. Thank you, Tara and Quinn!

chapter
five

It was Tuesday, five minutes till lunchtime, and Riley had spent most of the morning trying to track down Todd the Toad.

Where is he? Riley wondered. He hadn't shown up for English. His friend Joey had said it was because he had a dentist appointment.

Yeah, right, Riley thought. Todd probably knows I'm on a manhunt for him. I wouldn't be surprised if he spent the day hiding in the boys' room. That coward!

Riley headed over to the cafeteria. In the hall a guy from her English class came up to her. "Hey, Riley, do you want to—"

"No!" Riley barked and kept going.

All morning long, guys had been coming up to her and asking her out. The whole thing was a disaster. Everyone in school thought she was one of those girls who had no problems kissing just about anyone, anywhere, anytime. And it was all because of Todd Granger!

Michael-something from the basketball team sauntered up to her. "Hey, Riley—"

"No!" Riley marched into the cafeteria, totally furious. She headed toward the lunch line. Then she spotted Todd.

He was sitting at a table, wolfing down a huge bowl of chili. He was with three of his buddies.

Riley marched over to him. "I need to talk to you," she said. "Now. *Alone*."

The three guys smiled and got up. One of them slapped Todd on the back. "Good luck, dude," he said with a smirk.

Todd waved at Riley to sit down. "Hey, gorgeous. What's up? You look really hot in that—"

Riley remained standing. "I know what you're doing," she said in a low, angry voice. "And you'd better stop."

Now what should I do? Riley wondered. Start yelling at the top of my lungs? Pour his chili all over his khakis? What is the best way to make him understand that what he did was *not* cool?

Todd's face turned bright red. "What? What am I doing?"

Riley took a deep breath, then sat in the seat next to him. "Don't play stupid. You're lying to everyone about our date and telling them that we made out."

Todd smiled sheepishly. "We *did* kiss. So what if I was a little flexible with the truth?"

"Whatever. You need to get *un*-flexible with the truth

and tell everyone what really happened. As in, *nothing*!" Riley replied.

Todd glanced at his friends, who were sitting at the next table and watching the two of them. He turned back to Riley and shook his head. "Uh, I can't do that."

Riley resisted the urge to lunge at him. "What do you mean, you can't do that? Do you understand that about ten guys have asked me out in the last two days?"

"And that's a *bad* thing?" Todd said. "Dude, I did you a favor. You're popular!"

"I'm *popular* because you told a big fat lie about me," Riley barked. "Now, undo it!"

"I...I can't," Todd confessed. "That would make me look like a total dweeb. And I have a reputation to maintain." He added, "You should just chill out about all this. I bet it'll blow over in a week or two."

"'*Chill out*'?" Riley repeated. Blood was rushing to her head. Any second she was going to start throwing things. "'*Chill out*'? That is the lamest thing I've ever heard."

Riley realized that this was going nowhere. Todd was not going to do the right thing on his own. Well, she would have to do something about that.

Riley stood up to go. "You are a total toad," she told him. Then she turned to leave.

As she walked away, she heard Todd call after her, "Okay. Okay. I'll call you, Riley. We'll go out. I wouldn't pass up a date with *you*, Riley."

Riley realized just then that people were staring at

her. Lots of girls were pointing at her and whispering. Todd's buddies were whispering something, too, and cracking up.

Riley knotted her hands into fists as she walked away. This isn't the last of it, she promised herself. Todd the Toad had better watch out!

Chloe stared at herself in the mirror of the girls' bathroom. She dabbed on some lip gloss and frowned at her reflection.

"What's the matter?" Tara asked her as she brushed her hair. "Are you sick or something?"

"You look totally pale. You want to borrow my new blush?" Quinn asked, rummaging through her makeup bag.

Chloe shook her head. "No, thanks. I'm not sick or anything. It's just that...well, I'm kind of worried about Lennon."

"Why? I thought he asked you out three times after you blew him off," Tara said.

"Yeah," Chloe replied. "I told him last night that I couldn't go out with him till Thursday. Then he sent me three really sweet e-mails, and he tried to instant-message me again around eight. But I totally ignored them, just like it said in the Guide."

Quinn studied her purple nails. "Rule six, right? You have to wait at least six hours before returning his calls or e-mails."

"Yeah, that. I waited till this morning and I sent him

this supercasual e-mail." Chloe frowned. "But he hasn't written back yet. I checked on the library computer, like, half an hour ago."

"But this is *good* news," Tara said, patting Chloe on the arm. "It may seem like he doesn't care. But he really does."

"He's just giving you some space because he totally likes you and he doesn't want to suffocate you," Quinn added.

"Plus, he probably wants to act cool in front of his friends," Quinn pointed out. "He doesn't want to be a lovesick puppy."

"Even though he obviously is," Tara added with a wink.

"I thought he was a hunter and I was a bunny," Chloe said, confused. "Now he's a puppy?"

Quinn shrugged. "He's a hunter *and* a lovesick puppy," she explained.

"You're probably right," Chloe said. And she told herself to stop worrying so much about Lennon. Besides, she wanted to find Riley and talk to her right away. Todd had been spreading rumors about his date with Riley all over school. Chloe wasn't sure if her sister had been clued in yet.

"Chloe!"

Chloe turned around. Amanda rushed through the bathroom door. She looked totally panicked.

"What's the matter, Amanda?" Tara teased her. "Did

you get an A on your French quiz instead of an A plus, or what?"

"This is no joke!" Amanda cried out breathlessly. She whirled around to face Chloe. "You've got to help me. I'm in deep trouble!"

Chloe had never seen her friend look so freaked out. She was usually Ms. Calm, Cool, and Collected.

Something had to be wrong. Really wrong.

"What is it, Amanda? What?" she demanded.

chapter six

Amanda glanced in the direction of the bathroom door.

"What's wrong?" Chloe asked her. "Are you okay? Did something happen? Tell me!"

Amanda brushed her long brown hair out of her eyes and stepped closer to Chloe. "Bobby Flynn is out there," she said in a low, urgent voice. "You have to tell him that you and I have plans tonight."

"You and I have plans tonight?" Chloe asked, confused. "I thought we had plans for *tomorrow* night. That's Wednesday, right? I thought we were going to see a movie and—"

"No, no, no, no," Amanda said. "We don't have plans for tomorrow night. I mean, we *do*. But you have to tell Bobby they're for *tonight*."

"Huh?" Chloe, Quinn, and Tara said in unison.

"Come on, there's no time to waste," Amanda insisted.

She grabbed Chloe's arm and started dragging her out the door.

Out in the hall Bobby was leaning against a locker. He was wearing a West Malibu High basketball jersey and a pair of faded jeans that matched the color of his eyes. Chloe had to admit he was pretty cute.

"Hey, ladies," Bobby said with a smile.

"Uh, hi, Bobby," Chloe called out.

"Hey, Bobby," Tara and Quinn both said.

Bobby grinned at Amanda. "Amanda was just telling me, Chloe, that she and you are doing something tonight. But you've got to cancel whatever it is. I've got two tickets to the Crones concert, and I really want her to come with me."

[**Chloe**: **The Crones concert? That's, like, the hottest ticket in town. Amanda must be confused or something. There's no way she'd say no to that!**]

Chloe was about to tell Bobby that she had no problem canceling her plans with Amanda for tonight. But Amanda was staring at her with a desperate look in her eyes.

Chloe knew that look. It meant, "If you don't help me out here, I will never go to the mall with you *ever again*. Even if there's a killer sale at every single store in the place."

Lennon walked by just then with one of his friends.

He waved when he saw Chloe. Chloe waved distractedly back at him, then turned her attention to Bobby. She really wanted to say hi to Lennon. But she was in the middle of a minor crisis.

Chloe made herself smile at Bobby. "Oh, I am *so sorry*," she began. "But there's no way Amanda and I can cancel our plans. We're doing something special. Really, really, really special."

"Cool, can Quinn and I come?" Tara said eagerly.

"Yeah," Quinn said. "I'm not doing anything tonight. Well, except my math homework, but that can wait."

Chloe shook her head. "No! You wouldn't like what we're doing. It's something that, um, only Amanda and I would appreciate."

"Really? What is it?" Bobby asked her curiously.

Now what? Chloe thought. "It's—" she began, but she couldn't think of a good response.

"It's hard to explain," Amanda jumped in.

Chloe nodded. "Yes! We'll tell you guys all about it tomorrow."

Bobby shrugged. "Oh, well, too bad. Maybe another time." He gave Amanda a big, lovesick-puppy grin. "I'll call you later, okay, Amanda?"

"Bye," Amanda mumbled.

As soon as Bobby left, Tara turned to Amanda. "That guy is totally crushing on you!" she exclaimed.

"I know," Amanda said miserably. She sat down next to Chloe and covered her head with her hands. "That's the problem. Ever since I used the Guide on him yesterday he's been after me nonstop. I don't know how to get rid of him!"

"But why would you *want* to get rid of him? He's a hottie!" Quinn pointed out.

"He's sweet, but I kind of like guys with an IQ bigger than their shoe size," Amanda replied. "Still, the more I ignore him, and the more I don't return his calls and e-mails, the more he calls and e-mails."

Amanda looked at Tara and Quinn and sighed. "I don't want to admit it, but I think you guys were right about the Guide."

"Yes!" Quinn cheered.

"Now, don't ever question our wisdom again," Tara said with a grin.

Chloe nodded. With the results in from Amanda's experiment, she now knew for sure that the Guide was *the key* to dating success. And she knew exactly what she had to do to get Lennon right where she wanted him!

Lennon had stopped to talk to some friends in the hall. He glanced over his shoulder and smiled at Chloe. When she waved at him, he walked over.

"Hey, Chloe! I missed you in study hall today," Lennon said, touching her shoulder.

Chloe's heart melted. I *missed you, too*, she started to say. But she stopped cold.

Quinn was glaring at her with dagger eyes.

Tara mouthed the word *Guide*.

Chloe took a deep breath, then looked at Lennon with a stony expression. "Hey, Lennon. Yeah, well, I guess I was kind of busy."

Lennon didn't reply. He seemed confused—and a little hurt.

Chloe felt herself crumble a little. She wanted to follow the rules in the Guide, but she didn't want to make Lennon feel bad.

"Chloe, we'd better get going," Quinn told her. She adjusted her backpack strap and gave her a meaningful look.

"Yeah, let's get out of here," Tara piped up. "See you around, Lennon."

"I'll call you tonight, Chloe," Lennon said. "What time will you be home?"

Quinn grabbed Chloe's arm. "Come on, Chloe."

[<u>Chloe</u>: **Rule eight. Make sure he sees you hanging out with friends and busy with other activities. Make him think you're in demand.**]

"We are so, so busy!" Chloe said to Lennon, waving. "See you around!"

Chloe, Quinn, Tara, and Amanda headed down the hall. Once Lennon was out of sight, Tara and Quinn exchanged high fives.

"Chloe rules at the rules!" Tara cried.

"With a little help from my friends." Chloe smiled. "He said he'd call me, didn't he?"

"That's for sure," Quinn told her. "You've got the guy eating out of your hand!"

"I am so furious at Todd, I could punch him," Riley blurted out. "I wish I could get back at him. He needs a taste of his own medicine."

Riley's father, Jake Carlson, handed her a cup of steaming tea. "Calm down, buttercup. Drink this. It'll help. I made it myself. It's chamomile, rose hips, ginseng, echinacea, peppermint, spearmint, and burdock root, with a touch of blue-green algae and raw organic honey."

"Mmm, yum," Riley said sarcastically. She tried not to make a sour face. Ever since Jake and her mother, Macy, had separated, he had been eating weird foods, drinking weird teas, and acting...well, kind of *weird*.

Still, he seemed to enjoy his simple, solo trailer-park existence overlooking the clear-blue waters of the Pacific Ocean. He spent a lot of time meditating and doing yoga. He looked healthier than Riley had ever seen him.

Jake pulled a faded old "Be Here Now" sweatshirt over his T-shirt and sweatpants. "Okay, sweetie," he said. "Tell me what's going on with your life."

Riley took a deep breath and explained the whole story of Todd the Toad, from the ugly beginning to the even uglier end.

"Now every guy in school thinks I'm fast, loose, and out of control," Riley finished miserably. "Men! I hate them! Except for you, I mean," she added quickly. "And Manuelo, of course. The thing is, Todd has to pay for what he did to me. He has to be taught a lesson."

Jake held up his hand. "Whoa there, honey. Revenge is never the answer."

"But I'm really, really mad at him," Riley insisted. "Because of him, my reputation is totally ruined!"

Jake nodded understandingly. "I don't blame you for how you feel, pumpkin. But remember, don't place too much importance on what other people think of you. You know who you are inside. Let that shine through."

That *sounds* good, Riley thought. But what does it mean? "How do I do that?" she asked her father.

"First of all, get your feelings out of your system. Write all this stuff down, this stuff you've been telling me," Jake explained. "You should also try meditation. It will help you find some inner peace."

Inner peace. That sounded good, too, Riley thought. If she could only feel peaceful inside, it wouldn't matter what was going on outside of her. Nothing could touch her—not what other people said or did or thought about her.

"Here, I have some books you can borrow," Jake offered.

He got up and began searching through a messy stack of books with titles Riley had never heard of: *The Inner Journey to the Outer You, Serenity in Five Minutes a Day, The Joy of Carrots*.

"But, Dad," Riley complained. "I don't know if inner peace will work for me. I'm still liking the revenge idea—a lot."

Jake shook his head. "Believe me. Revenge isn't the way. Trust me, karma will work its magic on Todd. Karma means that what goes around comes around. Todd will get his just desserts eventually."

"How long is eventually?" Riley asked. "'Cause I'm not into waiting for it right now."

Jake laughed and pulled a book from his bookcase. "Ah, here we go." He handed Riley a dog-eared paperback. It was called *Meditating Your Way to Inner Peace*. He also gave her a book on deep breathing.

"This is what's going to work for you," Jake told her. "Deep breathing and meditating and focusing on yourself. Forget revenge."

Riley opened the meditation book to the first page. On it was a picture of a man in a really uncomfortable-looking position—legs crossed, bare feet over opposite knees, back stiff and straight. *That* was going to give her inner peace?

"Okay, Dad, I'll try it," Riley said. But deep down, she wasn't sure it would work.

Contrary to what her dad thought, revenge seemed like the right way to go. After all, Todd was an evil liar, and he had it coming to him. And if she, Riley Carlson, didn't stop him, he might turn around and do it again to someone else.

On the other hand, this inner-peace thing was kind of intriguing. It had worked for her dad so far. He had been a mess before he quit the fashion business. And now he seemed so happy and relaxed.

Revenge or inner peace—which was it going to be?

chapter
seven

On Wednesday night Riley stared at her face in the bathroom mirror as she brushed her teeth. She kept thinking about what her dad had told her. Inner peace. Maybe it *was* the answer.

She noticed something on her face. It was small and red and blotchy-looking.

"Oh great, a zit," Riley said with a sigh. It was probably from stressing about the toad. Maybe she *should* try the meditation thing. If nothing else, it might clear up her skin.

Riley finished up in the bathroom and went into her room. She lit some sandalwood incense that her dad had given her as well as a tall sage candle. Jake had told her that he always used incense and a candle during his meditation sessions.

Then Riley sat down on a cushion on the floor and opened the book *Meditating Your Way to Inner Peace*.

She read the instructions in the first chapter:

Get into a comfortable seated position. Close your eyes. Feel your breath moving in and out. Try to slow down the breathing so that you're inhaling on a count of eight, and exhaling on a count of ten.

Riley began to breathe in and out very loudly. She sounded like Darth Vader from *Star Wars*. "One, two, three," she counted. Hey, how are you supposed to breathe and count at the same time? she wondered.

When you've settled into a good breathing pattern, clear your mind of all thoughts. Say the "om" sound from deep within your belly. Draw the sound out like a chant. Repeat the chant again and again. Feel peace washing over you like a gentle rain. If thoughts enter your mind, place them in a fluffy white cloud and watch the cloud drift away.

"Okay, whatever," Riley said. She sat back and closed her eyes, took a deep breath, and began chanting. "*Ommmmmmmmmmmm.Ommmmmmmmmmmmm. Ommmmmmmmmmmm.*"

The sound made her throat vibrate and tickle. She

had to resist the temptation to crack up because she sounded so ridiculous.

But it was what the book said she had to do. Sit in a comfortable seated position, close her eyes, relax, breathe, and chant.

Oh, and clear her mind of all thoughts.

I wonder what Chloe is doing right now? Riley said to herself. I bet she and Lennon are out on a date, drinking lattes, staring into each other's eyes. Or maybe Chloe and Amanda are hanging out at the mall. Hey, I think they're having a sale at Sleek. I should be there with them! I really need some new skirts.

Riley shook her head. This wasn't how meditation worked. How was she going to find inner peace if she couldn't keep her mind totally blank?

Breathe, she told herself. Breathe. Be here now. I wonder if I have any new e-mails. Actually, who cares? I don't need other people right now. I especially don't need guys. I have inner peace.

The incense and candle were supposed to create a relaxing, spiritual atmosphere. Except that Riley didn't feel relaxed *or* spiritual right now.

I wonder how I did on that algebra exam today, Riley thought. Oh, and my poem is due on Friday! I still haven't found a good subject to write about. Let's see…I could write about flowers. I could write about thunderstorms. I could write about what a creep Todd is. I could write about meditation. Oops, I'm supposed to be meditating!

Riley took another deep breath and chanted again. With each breath and chant she felt more relaxed.

Then the thought of Todd came flooding back into her head.

I could fill his gym socks with itching powder. I could tape a "Kick Me" sign on his back. I could tell everyone he wears a wig.

"Riles, what are you *doing*?"

Riley's eyes flew open. Chloe was standing in the doorway.

"Oh, I'm meditating," Riley explained with a smile.

Chloe looked confused. "Why?"

"I don't know. Dad said it would be good for me," Riley explained. "He says I need to find inner peace instead of freaking out about Todd."

Chloe set her backpack down on the bed. "I still can't believe he did that to you! What a creep!"

"A total toad," Riley agreed.

Riley uncrossed her legs from her meditation position. She got up and hobbled over to the bed, next to her sister. Talking with Chloe was bound to be way more therapeutic than meditation!

They spent the next half hour ragging on Todd.

"Because of him, all these guys have been asking me out," Riley said when she'd finished complaining about Todd.

Chloe looked interested. "So who's been asking you out? Anyone cute?"

"Chloe!" Riley exclaimed. "That is not the point. Okay, maybe a few of them were cute. This one guy, Luke, was a hottie. But I said no to all of them! It was the right thing to do. These guys are just interested in me because of what Todd told them. They don't like me for who I am."

"I think you should get back at Todd big-time," Chloe suggested.

"I know," Riley replied. "But Dad thinks I should just let go of my anger and find serenity or whatever."

"Fine, then I'll get back at Todd *for* you," Chloe said, her eyes glittering.

Riley considered it. Then she shook her head. "No, don't do that. And don't you dare tell Todd any of this. I don't want to give him the satisfaction."

Chloe sighed. "Oh, okay."

Riley smiled at Chloe. "So. Enough about me. How are things going with Lennon?"

Chloe's face lit up. "I'm so glad you asked," she gushed. "He's totally great. I really, really like him. We're going out tomorrow, and I can't wait. We have so many things in common, you know? He likes pizza, and I like pizza. He's brilliant, and I'm—"

Just then the phone rang. Riley answered it. "Hello?"

"Oh, hey, this is Lennon. Is Chloe there?" said the voice on the other end.

Riley covered the mouthpiece with her hand. "It's Lennon."

Chloe turned pale. "Oh, uh…tell him I'm not here. Tell him I'm somewhere else. Tell him I'll call later," she whispered.

Riley was totally confused. "But—"

"Just do it!" Chloe whispered.

Riley relayed the message to Lennon. After she hung up, she said, "Chloe, why didn't you want to talk to him?"

"The Guide, *of course*," Chloe replied.

Sometimes her sister made no sense at all. "Guide? What guide?" Riley asked her.

"Well, I've been playing this thing with Lennon all wrong. I've been way too eager about hanging with him," Chloe explained. "Thank goodness Tara and Quinn told me about the Guide, or I would have lost him for sure! The Guide Website has all these amazing rules, like wait six hours before returning his calls and e-mails, don't kiss until the fourth date, don't tell him how you feel— stuff like that."

"Give me a break, Chloe. Lennon likes you for *you*. Why should you act differently just because Tara and Quinn and some Website say so?"

"You don't get it, Riley. The Guide works. I saw it work for Amanda. And it's already working for me!" Chloe insisted.

Oh, brother, Riley thought again. I am so glad I don't have a boyfriend right now. Meditating and inner peace are way better!

• • •

Chloe hit the Delete button for the sixth time and started composing yet another new e-mail.

```
Hey, Lennon. How's it going? I can't wait
to see you tomorrow night. It's been ages!
```

No, no, no, she told herself. Way too gushy! She hit the Delete button again.

```
Hey, Lennon. How's it going? I'm con-
firming our date for tomorrow after
school. Although if something has come
up for you, feel free to reschedule. We
could always get together next week or
the week after that. Whatever.
```

The phone rang. Chloe picked it up. "Hello?"

"Hey, Chloe." It was Lennon's familiar voice. Chloe's heart melted at the sound of it.

"Oh…hey," Chloe said. She wondered if Lennon had been expecting her to call back. "How's it going?"

"Great, how are you? What are you up to?"

[Chloe: Can I tell him that I've been sitting at the computer for the last hour trying to write the perfect e-mail for him? Probably not, huh? The Guide police would be after me in two seconds!]

"Oh, not much," Chloe replied. "What are you up to, Lennon?"

"I'm just reading that book you told me about—you know, the one about the guy who went backpacking all over California," Lennon said. "It's supercool. Thanks for recommending it."

Chloe felt a rush of pleasure. Lennon was reading a book she had mentioned to him. "No problem," she said eagerly. "I'm glad you like it. It made me want to go backpacking all over California, too."

"Yeah, me, too. Maybe we can do it together sometime."

Chloe was about to say, "Yes! What are you doing this weekend?" But she held her tongue. *Be the bunny*, she told herself sternly. "Yeah, I guess, maybe," she said in a noncommittal voice.

There was a brief silence on the other end. "So. What are you doing later?"

"Oh, nothing," Chloe replied. "Probably watching TV with my sister."

There was a longer silence this time. "Uh, Chloe?" Lennon said after a moment. "I thought you had plans tonight. That's why we couldn't go out."

Did I say that? Oops! How am I going to explain this one to him? Chloe thought, panicked.

"I...I did," Chloe stammered. "Have plans, I mean. With, um, Amanda. But they kind of got canceled at the last minute. I didn't think you'd be free anymore." That was kind of true, anyway. Amanda had canceled their movie plans because she had too much homework.

"Oh." Lennon sounded hurt.

"We're going to see each other tomorrow after school, anyway," Chloe reminded him brightly.

Chloe wanted to say more—like how much she missed him and how she was counting the seconds till their date. But I have to be tough, she thought. I can't stop following the Guide.

"Well, I've got to be going," Chloe told Lennon. "My sister needs the phone. I'll talk to you in school tomorrow, okay?"

There was another silence. "Um, okay. Bye," Lennon said slowly.

"Bye!" Chloe hung up the phone.

[Chloe: Don't look at me like that. What am I supposed to do? I'm not happy about having to treat Lennon like this. But it's for the good of our relationship. Dating is hard work! Sacrifices must be made!]

Still, Chloe felt as if she should do *something* to cheer up Lennon. On an impulse she rushed to the computer and deleted the last version of her e-mail to him. She wrote:

```
Dear Lennon,
I can't wait to see you tomorrow night.
```

```
I really, really miss you! You're the
sweetest guy I've ever met.
                      Love,
                      Chloe
```

Chloe took a deep breath and hit Send. Then a wave of doubt washed over her. In a panic she went to the Guide Website. She hit a link that said: WHAT TO DO WHEN YOU'VE BROKEN THE RULES.

She scrolled down the page until she found what she was looking for.

One of the most important rules in the Guide is Rule 2: Once you're dating a guy, don't gush or otherwise show him how you feel about him. If you break this rule, your relationship is as good as over. You might as well give up and start following the Guide with another guy.

Chloe read the paragraph over and over. Could it really be true? Could telling Lennon she missed him ruin their relationship forever?

chapter
eight

Riley closed her eyes and listened to the waves crashing against the rocks. It was six A.M. on Thursday, and she was meditating on the beach. Normally, sitting in pretzel position on the cold, wet sand in the early morning was not her idea of a good time. But it's what her father's book told her to do if the other meditation settings in the book didn't work.

Riley wasn't quite sure why she was doing this anyway. Meditation hadn't worked for her yesterday.

But her dad had warned her that it might take time. "Inner peace doesn't happen overnight," he had told her.

Riley breathed in the salty ocean air. For a minute or two her mind was a dark, blissful blank. Then thoughts began to crowd in. The thought of her poem, which was due tomorrow and which she still hadn't had much success with. The thought of a nice hot breakfast. Eggs. Pancakes. Bacon. O.J.

Riley's stomach grumbled. "All right, I'm giving up—for now," she said out loud.

She got up and started back toward her house. The sun was coming up, washing the sky in soft yellows and pinks. She took a deep breath. This was nice—walking alone along the beach, which was one of her favorite places in the world. For the moment she stopped thinking about the whole messed-up Todd situation.

Maybe *this* is inner peace, Riley thought.

Later at school Riley sat by herself in study hall and doodled in her notebook. She was aware of the students at the other tables, talking and laughing. She wasn't sure if they were talking and laughing about her. But it didn't matter. She, Riley Carlson, had inner peace.

Okay, maybe not.

Her good mood on the beach had lasted for about five whole minutes. Still, she was going to keep trying the meditation thing, as her dad had suggested. After all, it had been only two days.

She *did* feel a little better about the whole Todd business. She wasn't so furious at him anymore. But she still felt betrayed. *Alone* and betrayed. How could people trust Todd's version of Riley over *Riley's* version of Riley?

Then something clicked in her head.

It was an idea for a poem!

Riley opened her notebook to a fresh page. She began writing. For the next half hour Riley wrote…and wrote...and wrote. After days of writer's block she was unstoppable.

"I don't get it," Tara said at the mall after school on Thursday. "You followed rule number three, right? 'Don't accept a date with less than three days' notice'?"

"Yes," Chloe replied. "He asked me on Monday, and I said yes for tonight. That's three days—one, two, three." She counted on her fingers.

"And he canceled at the last minute?" Quinn asked. Chloe nodded miserably.

[**Chloe**: **Yes, I know it's Thursday. And I know I'm supposed to be on a date with Lennon instead of hanging out at the mall with Tara and Quinn. But Lennon canceled this afternoon. So now we're here trying to cheer me up. Which is not going to happen because I'm beyond cheering up!**]

"I don't get it," Tara repeated. "Are you sure you followed all the rules? How about number five, 'Never call him first unless it's to cancel a date'?"

"Or six, 'Wait at least six hours before returning his calls or e-mails,'" Quinn chimed in.

"You followed them all, right?" Tara demanded. "*Right*?"

Chloe squirmed. "Well...not exactly. I kind of broke the second rule."

"'Once you're dating a guy, don't gush or otherwise

show him how you feel about him'?" Quinn practically shouted. "Chloe, you *didn't!*"

"I did. I kind of wrote him this gushy e-mail last night," Chloe admitted.

Tara and Quinn stared at each other.

"This is a disaster," Tara said after a moment.

Quinn nodded. "Definitely."

The three girls headed into Banana Republic. Quinn went straight for a rack of black party dresses. "Follow me and keep talking," Quinn said to Tara and Chloe. "I do my best thinking while I'm shopping."

Tara and Chloe followed.

"Okay," Quinn said to Chloe as she thumbed through the rack. "Tell me *exactly* what you wrote him last night in your e-mail."

Chloe squirmed. "I think I wrote something about our date tonight. You know, like, I can't wait to see you, blah, blah, blah."

Tara shook her head. "That is not good. And how did you sign the e-mail? Initials or full name?"

Chloe squirmed some more. "Uh, I think I signed it Chloe. Or maybe…love, Chloe."

"Love!" Tara burst out. "That is a *major* Guide violation! No wonder Lennon canceled your date!"

"Thanks, you're really comforting me here," Chloe said sarcastically.

Quinn held up a short black halter dress. "How does this look?"

"Not now! We have a crisis," Tara said. "Let's get some smoothies and figure out how to fix it."

"Maybe it's not so bad," Chloe said. "Maybe he was canceling for a good reason."

"What did he say on your voice mail?" Quinn asked.

Chloe shrugged. "I don't remember. I think he said that something came up."

Tara patted her arm. "Poor Chloe."

Quinn gave Chloe a hug. "Come on. Let's get those smoothies."

The three girls left Banana Republic and headed over to Smashing Smoothies, which was next to the Cineplex. Tara ordered banana; Quinn ordered strawberry; and Chloe ordered raspberry. Then the three of them sat down on a bench next to some potted palm trees.

"Okay, damage-control time," Tara said. "I think Chloe's situation calls for rule eight."

"'Make sure he sees you hanging out with friends and busy with other activities,'" Quinn recited, slurping on her smoothie.

"I've already done that," Chloe reminded them.

"Hmm. Then maybe we need more drastic measures," Tara said.

"How about number nine?" Quinn said brightly.

Tara nodded. "Yes! 'If he compliments you on your jewelry, be vague about where you got it. Let him think it's from an old boyfriend.' Excellent suggestion, Quinn!"

"But I don't have any jewelry from old boyfriends,"

Chloe pointed out. "I have, like, a bunch of earrings and rings that I got from Riley and my parents and you guys. And my favorite turquoise choker and hand-beaded bracelet. That's it."

"Lennon doesn't have to know that," Quinn said pointedly.

Just then a familiar figure walked by. It was Todd the Toad! Chloe noticed that he had his arm around the shoulder of a cute blond girl. Chloe recognized her from school—Brynn or Britt or something like that.

"Hi, girls," Todd said with a smug little smile.

Chloe stared at Todd. She felt a rush of excitement that made her temporarily forget about Lennon. This was her opportunity. She could tell Brynn or Britt or whoever that Todd was a major liar. It was payback time for what he did to Riley!

Chloe started to stand. Then she sighed and sat back down again. After all, she had promised Riley. And she never broke promises.

Well, *almost* never.

"Hi, Todd," Chloe said cheerfully. "How's it going? Didn't I see you at the Newsstand last Friday night? You were out with my sister, right?"

Maybe she couldn't come right out and blab on Todd. But she could make him sweat for a few minutes.

Todd turned pale. "Uh, yeah. Maybe. Come on, Brynn, the movie is starting in five minutes." He grabbed her arm and started to yank her away.

Chloe loved watching Todd squirm. "Don't go yet! I want to hear every detail about your date with my sister, and I'm sure that Brynn would love to hear about it, too!" She laughed as she watched Todd practically drag Brynn into the Cineplex.

Then Chloe stopped. She spotted Lennon walking toward the theater entrance, too. Her heart skipped a beat. He looked really cute in his jeans and turquoise T-shirt. His hair was perfectly spiked, as always.

And then she did a double-take. What was he doing here? He was supposed to be out on a date—with her!

All of a sudden a girl caught up to Lennon. She said something to him, and the two of them laughed. He grabbed her hand, and she smiled up at him.

Chloe felt her heart breaking into a million tiny pieces. Lennon had broken a date with her to go out with another girl.

I guess the Guide was right, Chloe thought. Lennon and I are as good as over.

chapter nine

Chloe couldn't stop starring at them. Lennon was on a date with another girl! Chloe didn't know the girl's name, but she recognized her from West Malibu High. She had long curly red hair, and she was wearing a denim skirt and pink top that showed off her athletic-looking body.

Just before the two of them entered the Cineplex, Lennon happened to turn around. His gaze fell on Chloe and her friends. He looked totally surprised.

Chloe met his eyes. But she had to look away after a second. Otherwise, she might start crying in front of him, in front of her friends, in front of every single person at the mall.

Todd had taken the opportunity to slither away with his date. Tara and Quinn both grabbed Chloe's arm.

"*What* is Lennon doing with that girl?" Tara whispered. "Who is she?"

Chloe shook her head. She couldn't bring herself to answer. *Lennon is on a date with a really cute girl who isn't me.*

"I...I don't know," Chloe managed to say finally.

"This is totally serious," Quinn said. "Way more than we thought."

"It's that e-mail you sent him last night," Tara declared. "This is what happens when you don't follow the Guide."

"We need help," Quinn stated. "Let's check out that teen dating Website again. I think they have a special page for dating emergencies."

"I don't think the Guide can help me now," Chloe moaned. "Lennon's already got another girlfriend! I can't believe it!"

"She is not his girlfriend. It's just a dumb movie date," Tara said. "He's probably just trying to make you jealous."

Quinn nodded. "Tara's right. Guys are way into playing games."

"Come on, come on," Tara said, dragging Chloe toward a computer and office supply store. "We need Internet access now!"

Chloe followed along, but her heart and mind were a million miles away. Or a few feet away, anyway—inside the Cineplex, where Lennon was sharing a cozy bucket of popcorn in the dark with someone else.

● ● ●

Riley sipped her latte and stared at the words she'd written in her notebook. "'Loneliness,'" she read. "Or should it be 'solitude'?"

She and Larry were hanging out together at the Newsstand. Riley was trying to finish her poem, which was due tomorrow.

Across the table Larry clapped his hands. "Yes!" he exclaimed.

Riley glanced up. "Yes, what?" she asked. "Loneliness or solitude?"

Larry looked confused. "Yes as in 'Yes, that babe over there is really hot,'" he said, nodding at a girl who was sitting a few tables away.

Riley sighed and shook her head.

She had to admit, though, it was kind of nice hanging out with Larry. She hadn't seen many of her friends this week. Sierra was still out sick with the flu, her sister was busy with her Lennon problems, and the rest of the kids in school—well, Riley was beginning to have the feeling that they didn't get what she was about. Not one bit. Not if they could believe what Todd had said about her.

Riley put down her pen. "Larry, don't you think you should judge people based on who they are rather than what they look like? Isn't it what's inside that counts? You should really think about taking up meditation and finding inner peace—"

Riley stopped short. A guy was walking onto the

stage of the Newsstand, holding a guitar. He had chest-nut-brown curls that fell to his chin and a tall, lanky body. The guy slipped on a brown ski cap and sat on the stool onstage.

Whoa. Is this guy hot or what? Riley thought.

A cheer went up in the room. Obviously, the guy was popular. He leaned in to the microphone and began strumming an edgy-sounding ballad on his guitar. After a few bars he began singing:

"In my room,
All alone,
I don't even want to pick up the telephone
Because I can't relate,
I can't communicate,
Not since that day you walked out into the rain."

Larry nodded at the guitar player. "Dude, who wears hats like that anymore?" he whispered to Riley.

Riley frowned. "Larry, that guy is up there sharing his pain, expressing his feelings, and all you see is his hat?"

"Hey, you're the child of fashion designers, you should be noticing these things, too," Larry said.

"*Shhhhhh!*" Riley hissed.

She wanted to concentrate on the guitar player and his amazing voice. And his amazing face. And his eyes. And his mouth. And…

[**Riley**: Okay, I admit it. It's hard not to judge people by their appearance sometimes. But this guy is beyond cute. And I really admire the way he opens up emotionally through his art. Really!]

After the set was over, Larry stood. "I've got to go and finish my algebra homework," he said. "You want to walk home together?"

Riley was about to say yes. Then she glanced at the guitar player and shook her head. "No, I think I'll stick around here for a bit."

"Okay, see you later." Larry took off.

Riley stared at the guitarist for a few moments. She really wanted to talk to him. She really wanted to know if he wrote his own songs.

She took a deep breath, summoning the courage. It wasn't every day she just walked up to a stranger and started gabbing with him.

The guitar player was leafing through some dog-eared sheet music and drinking an espresso. He glanced up when Riley approached him. "Hey," he said.

"Hey," Riley said in a shy voice. "Um, I really liked your songs."

"Thanks." The guy smiled. "I'm Nick, by the way."

"I'm Riley. Riley Carlson," she said. "So, you come here often?"

Ugh! That sounded totally lame, Riley said to herself.

"As often as I can. I need the money," Nick replied with a grin.

"You were great. Especially that song about people who buy jeans with the holes already in them."

She noticed that Nick gave a quick glance at her jeans.

Riley looked at them, too. She had one perfect hole in each knee.

"Oh. I really didn't buy these like that," she explained quickly. "I made the holes myself. I mean, they came naturally," she added. "You know, with time. I'm not a princess or anything."

> [<u>Riley</u>: **What do you think? Should I keep going or end this topic *before* I humiliate myself beyond recognition?**]

"Well, anyway, I really liked that song," Riley said. "Did you write it yourself?"

Nick nodded. "I write all my own stuff."

Riley hesitated, then said, "You know, I do a little writing, too. Right now I'm working on something for English class. I go to West Malibu High."

"What do you write? One of those summer vacation essays?" Nick teased her. "Sorry, that came out wrong."

Riley blushed. "No! Well, I did write a summer vacation essay once, about our family trip to Yosemite. We saw a bear. I mean, it was because my dad had left the food out, but—" She shook her head. She had to stop babbling. "Never mind the bear. I'm actually, um, writing poetry these days."

Nick looked interested. "Really? Cool. I love writing poetry. I mean, that's what my song lyrics are, basically."

Riley felt a rush of excitement. Nick, an almost-famous musician, was actually talking to her about poetry! This was a big deal, especially since most of the people in her English class seemed to think that poetry was boring.

And then she felt a twinge of embarrassment. She'd been complaining about guys judging her based on things like looks and reputation; Todd thought she was hot A-crowd dating material, and Malcolm thought she was, well, what Todd had told him she was.

Now here was Nick, whom she'd judged on the outside, too. She'd thought he was a hot-looking rocker. But he seemed to be way more than that.

"Well, I'm not as good as you, but maybe someday..." Riley shrugged and smiled. "I guess I'd better go. It was nice talking to you. I'll watch for your first CD."

"I'll be back here tomorrow if you'd rather catch it live. And if you want to hang out, my set will end at nine," Nick added.

Ohmigosh. He's asking me out. Sort of, Riley thought.

"Uh..." Riley said.

"What? Past your curfew?" Nick joked. "Don't worry, I'm sixteen. I have a curfew, too."

Riley laughed. "I'll be here."

And then an awful, terrible thought occurred to her.

What if Nick had heard about her from Todd? Was *that* why he was asking her out?

"*Hey!*" Riley cried out, punching Nick on the arm.

"Ow! Hey, what?" he said, rubbing his arm.

"Have you been talking to Todd Granger?" Riley demanded.

Nick frowned. "Todd *who*?"

Riley clamped her hand over her mouth.

[Riley: Oops, big mistake. Nick has no idea who Todd the Toad is. He actually likes me for me. Plus, I think I just damaged his guitar-playing arm.]

Riley smiled nervously. "Oh, nothing. Nobody. Mistaken identity. Gotta go, see you tomorrow!"

Nick rubbed his arm again and smiled. "Don't forget!" he called after her.

chapter
ten

"**G**o ahead, Larry," Mr. Camino encouraged him. "Let's hear your poem."

It was Friday in English class. Larry walked up to the front of the room. He glanced at Riley for a second. He looked nervous. Riley gave him a thumbs-up.

Larry ran a hand through his spiky brown hair, then began to read from a piece of paper:

> "I love the Lakers,
> They are so cool.
> Shaq O'Neal and Kobe Bryant,
> They really rule.
> I want to be like Magic
> And also Kareem.
> I want to score points
> And be the star of the team."

Larry took a bow. Everyone in the class clapped. "Lakers rule!" someone shouted.

"Lakers!" Larry replied, raising his fist in the air.

"Uh, thank you, Larry," Mr. Camino said. He peered around the room. "Riley, why don't you go next?"

Riley felt her heart skip a beat. It was show time! She had been working really hard on her poem. She hoped Mr. Camino—and the rest of the class—would like it.

She walked up to the front of the class and began to read:

"Solitude is one thing,
Loneliness is another.
Solitude is when I'm walking along the beach
And I'm happy just breathing and being.
Loneliness is when not even the beach
Can comfort me or keep me company.
Still, it's the loneliness that makes me grow
While it's the solitude that keeps me whole."

"Wonderful, Riley," Mr. Camino said. He looked impressed. "Class? Any comments or observations?"

"Um, I think maybe she needs to see the guidance counselor," a boy named J.R. suggested.

Larry raised his hand. "No, dude, it's not like that at all. I think that Riley's poem is about the *Clippers*! Remember that season when they were way last? But they hung in there and kept going!"

Riley sighed. Great. No one understands my poem! I might as well be from another planet. Oh, well, at least Mr. Camino likes it.

Mr. Camino called on Todd to read his poem next. Riley's stomach churned at the sight of him. Inner peace, she reminded herself. Inner peace.

Todd smoothed out a crumpled piece of notebook paper and began to read:

"There once was a girl,
Her name was RC.
She called me all the time.
I told her to wait in line,
But she wouldn't let up on me,
So we went on a date
And the rest is history."

Riley felt her cheeks burn bright red. Several students in the class started cracking up. A few of them even whistled at her!

Riley couldn't believe that Todd had the nerve to lie about their date—and then lie about it again, in a poem, in front of her and the rest of the class! Did his evil have no end?

Forget inner peace. Inner rage was more like it! And it was time Riley did something about it! She had to get him, and get him good. But how?

● ● ●

Chloe leaned against her locker, fiddling with her combination. She was trying not to stare at Lennon, whose locker was right across and a few doors down from hers. Amanda and Riley were standing next to her.

"Just *talk* to him," Riley whispered.

"Yeah," Amanda agreed. "Ask him what was up with that other girl last night."

Chloe had filled in Riley and Amanda on the whole mall fiasco. Like Tara and Quinn, Amanda had been supersympathetic. She hadn't even given her a hard time about breaking the rules in the Guide.

"I can't," Chloe replied. "That would be violating rule ten: 'If you see him hanging out with another girl, don't ask him who she is or act as if you care. Act super-confident and secure!'"

Riley shook her head. "Chloe, don't you get it? These rules did the opposite of what you wanted. Because of the rules, you've been acting like you don't like him all week. Who can blame him for asking someone else out?"

"But the rules worked for Amanda and Bobby!" Chloe reminded her, trying to keep her voice low. She turned to Amanda. "You said it yourself, right?"

"I was wrong. The rules *didn't* work for me and Bobby. Bobby told me yesterday that he's had a crush on me since I transferred to West Malibu. He's been waiting to ask me out all this time!" Amanda explained.

"What?" Chloe gasped.

"It was just a coincidence that he asked me out," Amanda went on. "I'm still trying to let him down. I know he's cute and popular and everything, but I really just want to be friends."

"So what I'm hearing you say is that the Guide *didn't* work for you," Chloe murmured.

Amanda nodded. "Exactly."

Chloe's head was pounding. She tried to digest Amanda's words. The rules hadn't worked for Amanda at all. It was just a coincidence that Bobby had asked Amanda out when he did.

Did that mean the rules hadn't been working for Chloe, either? Instead of making Lennon even crazier about her with her ice-princess act, maybe she had just *driven* him crazy—and then driven him away!

She told all this to Riley and Amanda. "What do you think? I know what Tara and Quinn would say. 'Have faith in the Guide!'"

Amanda sighed. "Why don't you just talk to the guy?"

Chloe hesitated. "I—I don't know. That sounds kind of scary."

"What have you got to lose?" Riley asked.

"Good point," Chloe agreed.

Chloe glanced over at Lennon. At the exact same moment he turned around and glanced at her.

Their eyes locked. Oh, Lennon, Chloe thought. Did I blow things big-time? If I did, I am so sorry!

Chloe started to walk across the hall and talk to him—for real.

But then the redheaded girl rushed up to Lennon. "Hey, Lennon," she said in a honey-sweet voice and put her hand on his arm.

Chloe's heart sank all the way down to her strappy sandals. She felt tears well up in her eyes, and she had to turn around to keep Lennon from seeing them.

It's totally hopeless, she thought. I've lost Lennon forever.

chapter
eleven

As Nick strummed away on his guitar and sang a song about fashion victims, Riley bent her head over her notebook and worked on her new poem:

> Mr. Toad, what are you afraid of?
> Why do you lie and run?
> Do you think girls won't like you?
> Do you think guys will make fun?

Riley took a long sip of her decaf mocha. She knew this poem wasn't going anywhere. But it felt good to get all the anger and bad feelings about Todd the Toad out of her system.

It was Friday night, and the Newsstand was packed. Chloe, Tara, Quinn, and Amanda were sitting at a table in the corner. There were a bunch of other kids from West Malibu High, too.

Across the room Todd was hanging out with a couple of guys that Riley didn't know.

Riley tried hard to ignore him, but it wasn't easy. Todd was gesturing wildly with his arms and laughing loudly. Riley thought it was kind of rude since someone was performing.

Nick finished up his song with a couple of crashing chords. The room broke into applause.

"Thank you. I'm going to take a short break, and I'll be right back!" he announced.

He set his guitar down and came up to Riley's table. "Hey, what are you doing? Writing another essay about Yosemite?" he teased her.

Riley grinned. "Nope. I'm working on a new poem," she said.

Nick looked interested. "Really? Could I take a look?" he asked.

Riley slid the piece of paper across the table. "Sure. I have two more lines to go," she said. "And it's not very good. But sure, whatever."

Riley felt a little nervous about showing the unfinished poem to Nick, especially after the way her English class had reacted to the one she had written about solitude.

But Nick was smiling as he read her Todd poem. "This is awesome," he said after a minute. "You should write song lyrics!"

Riley beamed. "Really? Wow, thanks."

"I mean it, this poem would make a great song," Nick went on.

[**Riley**: Then it came to me. Remember when Dad said something about leaving karma to take care of Todd? What goes around, comes around. Well, I just thought of a little way to help karma speed things along.]

Chloe stabbed a fork into her peanut-butter pie. She was sitting at a table at the Newsstand with her friends. "The Guide totally *ruined* my relationship with Lennon," she muttered darkly.

"*What*?" Tara and Quinn said in unison.

The music in the Newsstand was really loud. Some cute guy with a guitar was singing about fashion victims. Chloe wondered briefly how someone could be a fashion victim. Fashion *hero* was more like it. But her thoughts returned all too soon to the subject at hand: the Guide.

"I said, the Guide totally *ruined* my relationship with Lennon!" Chloe repeated louder.

"The Guide did *not* ruin your relationship," Tara insisted. "The rules worked for Amanda and Bobby. Don't worry, Chloe. You'll see. They'll work for you and Lennon, too."

"Yeah. Just as soon as he gets rid of that other girl," Quinn added. "Chloe, are you finished with that pie?"

Her hand slid across the table toward Chloe's dessert.

"No!" Chloe said, hugging the plate protectively. "I've lost the love of my life. Don't take my peanut-butter pie away, too!"

"Guys," Amanda said in a patient voice. "I said it once, and I'll say it again. The Guide did not work for Bobby and me. He told me in plain English that he's had a big crush on me for ages. It was just a coincidence! That's all!"

"There are no such things as coincidences when it comes to dating," Tara said.

> [Chloe: That's when a lightbulb went off in my head. Actually, it was more like one of those huge spotlights you see in baseball stadiums. WHEN WAS THE LAST TIME EITHER TARA OR QUINN HAD A DATE?]

Chloe leaned across the table. "Hey, Tara. I was just wondering, when was the last time you went out with a guy?" she asked sweetly.

Tara stopped drinking her chai mid-gulp. "Huh? What? Oh, I don't know, like, recently."

"Like six months ago, I think," Quinn reminded her with a smirk.

Chloe whirled around on Quinn. "And you? When was the last time *you* had a date? Wasn't it, like, a year ago or something?"

Quinn blushed. "No way!" she said in a huffy tone.

"It was more like…more like…eleven *months* ago."

Chloe sighed. I should have listened to Amanda, she thought. For that matter, I should have listened to my own sister. She told me the rules were stupid. And they are!

Quinn, Tara, and Amanda started another round of arguments about the rules. While they argued, Chloe noticed a familiar figure walk into the Newsstand.

Lennon.

He took a table by himself in the corner. Then he pulled a book out of his backpack. Chloe realized that it was the book about California backpacking—the one she'd told him to read.

Her heart did a somersault. It was time to make things right. H*er* way, not Tara's way or Quinn's way or anyone else's way.

Chloe got up from her chair.

"Where are you going?" Tara asked her.

"To apologize to Lennon," Chloe said.

"No!" Tara and Quinn cried out at the same time.

"Yes, and you can't stop me," Chloe said. "Amanda, don't let them follow me. Spill cappuccino all over them if you have to."

Amanda giggled. "Totally."

"Chloe, that's so mean!" Quinn protested.

Chloe walked across the room to Lennon's table. When he saw her, he put his book down and stood up. "Uh, hey. Hi," he said, sounding nervous.

"Hi. Can I join you?" Chloe asked him.

Lennon nodded. "Sure."

Chloe sat down across from him. "I wanted to come over and apologize. I've been acting like a real jerk all week," she began.

Lennon looked surprised. "What do you mean?"

Chloe explained about how much she liked hanging with him and how much she hadn't wanted to blow things with him.

"But I thought you didn't like me anymore," Lennon said when she had finished. "You didn't return my calls or e-mails. You weren't as sweet and nice as you used to be. You made up some bogus excuse about being busy Wednesday night, when all you were doing was watching TV with your sister. I thought you were giving me a hint."

Chloe winced. "I know. That's totally my fault. I thought *you* wouldn't like *me* anymore if I kept acting like that. Like I liked you, I mean."

Lennon frowned. "Huh? That doesn't make any sense."

Chloe smiled. "I know. It doesn't make any sense at all."

She scooted back her chair and stood up. "Anyway, I'm sorry. If you don't want to go out again, I totally understand. But if you ever do—"

"Yes!" Lennon said immediately. "What are you doing now? Like tonight?"

Chloe smiled. Inside, she felt a huge *whoosh* of

relief—and happiness. Everything was good between them again!

And then she did something. She broke rule number seven—right in front of Tara and Quinn and everyone else in the Newsstand.

She grabbed Lennon and kissed him on the lips.

Across the room she heard a whistle. "Way to go, Chloe!" Amanda cheered.

chapter
twelve

It was Saturday night and the Newsstand was more crowded than Riley had ever seen it.

Sitting near the stage were at least two dozen kids from West Malibu High: Amanda, Bobby, Tara, Quinn, Todd, Larry, and a bunch of others. Chloe and Lennon were sitting at a table by themselves, in the back. They were holding hands and sharing a big latte.

Riley was pacing around the room, a bottle of sparkling water in hand. She wished she could calm down. But she was so nervous. Could she and Nick pull this off?

[Riley: Maybe if I'd kept up with the meditating, I wouldn't be here right now. On the other hand, Nick thinks I have a brilliant future as a writer. I guess life is all about trade-offs: Inner peace versus really cool, edgy song lyrics.]

Nick stepped up onto the stage and began tuning the strings of his guitar.

Riley thought he looked especially cute tonight in a faded denim shirt and jeans.

Stop it with the "cute" stuff, Riley told herself. He's about more than cute. He's an awesome musician. He appreciates poetry. He's nice. He's funny. And he's…he's really cute.

Nick tapped on the microphone. "How're you all doing tonight?" he called out. Feedback buzzed and echoed from the speakers.

Everyone clapped. "Lakers rule!" Larry called out.

"Right on," Nick replied. He strummed a chord on his guitar. "This is a brand-new song I wrote with a good friend of mine. She wrote the lyrics and I wrote the tune. It might be kind of familiar to some of you—especially those of you who hail from West Malibu High."

"West Malibu High rules!" Larry yelled. He and Bobby exchanged high fives.

Riley hunched up against a post in the corner and took a long swig of her sparkling water. *This is it*, she thought.

Nick strummed a few more chords, then began singing:

"Mr. Toad, what are you afraid of?
Why do you lie and run?
Do you think girls won't like you?
Do you think guys will make fun?

"Your love life is so boring,
You have to fake it for the crowd.
You said you kissed her when you didn't.
You told all kinds of tales out loud.

"Mr. Toad, what are you afraid of?
Mr. Toad, what are you afraaaaaaid of?"

Nick kept singing, but he was smiling at Riley. Riley smiled back at him.

People in the audience began cracking up. Some of them stared and pointed at Todd.

Even in the dimly lit café, Riley could see that Todd was blushing. He looked totally humiliated and was squirming in his chair.

Now you know how it feels, Riley thought.

[**Riley**: **So my dad was right. The karma thing does work. In the end Todd got what he deserved for his meanness. Of course, I kind of helped move Todd's karma along a little bit. But I'm sure Dad will understand!**]

After the set was over, Nick came up to Riley. He winked at her. "How did I do?" he asked her.

"Great!" Riley said. "Thank you so much for setting my silly lyrics to music. The results were exactly what I wanted!"

She glanced over her shoulder. Todd was slinking

out the front door, his head hung low. He didn't even look at her.

"Silly lyrics?" Nick repeated. "They're not silly at all. In fact, I'd like to keep singing 'Mr. Toad' at my gigs—with your permission, that is."

"Oh, wow, cool," Riley said.

Nick touched her hair. "*You're* cool, Riley. I guess there's more to the Malibu princess than meets the eye."

Riley blushed and smiled. She didn't know what to say. She hadn't been this happy in a long time—well, all week, anyway. She just wanted to freeze this moment in time. And freeze Nick's hand right there where it was touching her hair.

"Hey, what are you doing later?" Nick asked Riley, breaking her happiness trance. "There's a party after the set. You want to come?"

Riley glanced at her watch. Nine P.M. "Uh...what time is the party?" she asked since her curfew was eleven sharp.

Nick laughed. "Ten," he said. "It would be fun to hang out with you. Plus, I'd love to get some feedback from you on some lyrics I've been working on."

"Sure," Riley said with a grin.

Now all she had to do was get Chloe to cover for her—just in case she was late.

Chloe blinked into the darkness as the bedroom door creaked open. She glanced at the digital alarm clock. It said: 12:03 A.M.

Riley tiptoed through the doorway. "It's me," she whispered.

Chloe sat up in bed. "How was it? How was your big date with the rock star?" she whispered back.

Riley sat down on the bed next to Chloe and giggled. "He is *not* a rock star. Yet."

"Well, he's supercute, whatever he is," Chloe said. "I covered for you. Mom thinks you're in there." She pointed to a lumpy figure in Riley's bed. "It's your old comforter."

"And Mom believed *that*?" Riley asked.

Chloe shrugged. "I guess. Anyway. She's asleep and so is Manuelo."

"Excellent. Thanks!" Riley said.

Chloe hugged her knees to her chest. Even in the darkness she could tell by the look in Riley's eyes that her sister was really happy. "Great date?"

"Great date," Riley said, nodding. "How about you?"

Chloe grinned. "Better than great. Lennon is such an awesome guy. I'm so glad I dropped those silly rules and started acting like myself again!"

"I *told* you the Guide was stupid," Riley said, wagging her finger.

Chloe gave Riley a mock salute. "Yes, ma'am. From now on I'll *always* listen to you."

Riley laughed. "Yeah, right."

Chloe giggled, too. "Well, maybe not *always*. Hey, let's make a deal. We should listen to each other *some-*

times. But as far as everyone else goes, let's not follow other people's programs anymore. No dating rules, no meditation manuals, nothing."

"Good idea!" Riley agreed. "Although that meditation stuff isn't bad. You should try it with me sometime."

"*Ommmmmm*," Chloe chanted.

Riley smiled. "Hey, get up. Let's celebrate our new beginning with some double-chocolate mint fudge from the fridge."

"Maybe tomorrow," Chloe said. "You may be into partying till midnight. But I'm tired."

[<u>Chloe</u>: So Riley and I sealed the deal by making a date to go to the mall tomorrow. Nothing says "new beginnings" like new clothes. That's Chloe Carlson's rule number one!]

mary-kate olsen **ashley** olsen

so little time

Chloe
and Riley's

SCRAPBOOK

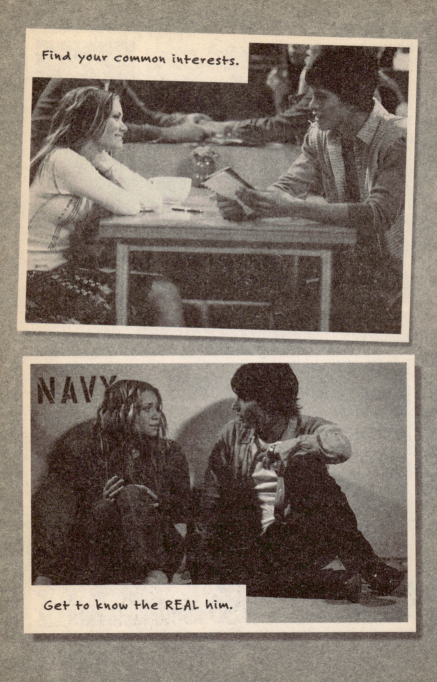

Find your common interests.

Get to know the REAL him.

Here's a sneak peek at

so little time

Book 11
boy crazy

Riley checked her hair in the reflection of the glass door before she entered Starbucks.

I've got to look good, she thought nervously. Majorly good. Good enough to make up for the fact that I'm not French, not famous, and not the daughter of Jacques D'Oisseau.

In her low-rise brown jeans and orange knit top, Riley thought she'd probably pulled it off. The outfit was totally cute and hip. And her hair had been in a good mood this morning. It fell perfectly around her face.

"Hi," Marc Hudson said, standing up the minute he saw her.

Good manners! Riley loved that.

Marc was wearing a white T-shirt under an unbuttoned black cotton shirt. And jeans. Plus he had a small woven leather necklace with a turquoise bead around his neck — just like the one Riley was wearing.

He looked amazing.

"Hi," Riley said, tilting her head so that her hair swung back and forth a little.

"Great necklace," Marc said, shooting her a smile the minute he noticed it.

"Thanks," Riley said with a grin. "It's my favorite because no one else has one like it."

Marc laughed and gestured toward the cup of coffee on his table. "I got here early," he explained. "I needed a double espresso big-time. What can I get you?"

"I guess I'll have a cappuccino," Riley said.

Marc did a double take. "Seriously?"

Uh, yeah, Riley thought. Why not? "Is that a problem?" she asked.

"Oh." He shrugged. "I'm just surprised. I mean, I guess you've been in America so long, you're picking up bad habits."

Bad habits? Drinking cappuccino? Riley frowned and shook her head, as if she didn't get it.

"Well, you grew up in France, right?" Marc said. "None of the Europeans I know drink cappuccino for anything other than breakfast."

They don't? Who knew? Riley thought, feeling a little silly.

She tried to act as if she'd known that all along. "Yeah, I've picked up some pretty bad habits since I've been here," she mumbled, blushing.

Like lying about who I am! Riley said to herself.

But she was going to correct that problem right

away. Just as soon as she could find the right spot in the conversation.

Marc went up to the counter and got her a cappuccino. Then he sat down, leaned forward, and said, "Okay, so tell me everything about you."

Everything about me? Riley thought. You mean, like starting with the fact that my name is really Riley Carlson, not Danielle?

Riley tried to think of how to word it, but her throat closed up and her mind went blank. She didn't know where to begin.

"No, you go first," she said finally.

Marc nodded. "Okay."

Quickly he told her that he was an only child. That he'd grown up in New York City. And that he was now a junior at a private school there.

"And besides that, I love the beach—"

"I do, too!" Riley interrupted.

"And hip-hop music, especially Master Crush," Marc went on. "And I'm a total zombie in the morning. And that's everything you need to know about me."

"That's incredible," Riley said.

"How come?" Marc asked.

"Well, I *adore* the beach," Riley said. "And I'm a complete maniac about Master Crush. And I get really cranky if I don't get enough sleep."

"Wow. It's like you're my twin or something," Marc said, grinning.

Riley almost burst out laughing. You have no idea how funny that is! she thought. She had to bite her tongue to keep from saying, "I already have a twin!"

"Anyway, I thought about going skiing in France for spring break," Marc said. "But I'm glad I came here instead."

"Skiing? Really? Would there be enough snow at this time of year?" Riley asked.

Marc stared at her.

Oops. I'm supposed to *know* the answer to that if I grew up in France! Riley realized.

"I mean, with global warming and everything," she added really fast. "We've had to cut way back on our spring skiing *back home*."

"Yeah." Marc eyed her strangely. "But anyway, my dad really wanted me to come out here. He's trying to get me to spend more time with him."

"That's nice," Riley said.

Wow. He's so easy to talk to, she thought. She was having such a great time, she hated to spoil the mood by saying, "Oh, by the way, I'm not who you think I am."

"Hey, you want to go hang out at the beach?" Marc asked suddenly.

"Sure." Riley took one last sip of her cappuccino.

This is so much fun! she thought.

But I've got to tell him…soon.

They headed to the beach, and as they walked past her house, Riley tried not to glance up at the deck.

What if Manuelo sees me? she thought. He might call her by her real name.

"So anyway, Danielle, what's the deal with the commercial your dad is shooting?" Marc asked. "Are you totally pumped about it?"

"Well, uh…" Riley sputtered.

Tell him now, she thought. Just say it—he's *not* my dad. He's just the guy who rented a house down the beach from us.

But Marc didn't wait for an answer. He just kept rambling on about how much he loved Jacques's movie, *Tunnel of Rain*. How he had seen it shown as a Classic Re-release at the Cannes Film Festival in Nice last year. And how he was hoping to hang out at the commercial shoot later this week.

Riley glanced up. They were coming to Jacques's beach house. She walked a little faster.

"I am so into your dad," Marc said. "I mean, I've heard that this commercial is going to be really cool. People say it's going to be shot in black and white, right? And sort of look like an old detective movie from the 1940s?"

Riley had no idea. This was it. She couldn't fake it anymore. "To tell you the truth," Riley said, "Jacques is not my father."

Marc's head snapped up. "Huh?"

"You made a mistake," Riley explained. "My name is Riley Carlson—not Danielle. I'm not Jacques D'Oisseau's daughter."

"Are you serious?" Marc looked shocked. And maybe disappointed. Riley couldn't tell.

He stopped walking and just stood there on the beach. Riley stared at the sand as the water almost swooshed on his sneakers.

"Yeah," Riley started to say. "It was a mistake. I..." She was about to explain the whole thing to him.

But just then she heard a high-pitched bark. Then she saw a little tan dog bolt down the steps of Jacques's house and onto the sand.

"Chaudette!" Riley called, running to catch the puppy. "Chaudette! Come back!"

The puppy stopped when she heard Riley calling her name. For a minute, she just wagged her tail. Then she turned and trotted back to Riley.

"Sorry," Riley called to Marc. "Hang on a minute. I've got to put her inside."

Riley hurried up the steps of Jacques's house. Marc followed her as she opened the sliding glass door just a few inches and dropped the puppy inside.

"Now, you stay where you belong, understand?" Riley said.

She closed the door and turned to see Marc standing beside her. He gazed in through the glass door—toward the fireplace mantel.

Sitting right there, on top, was a Golden Globe Award.

Marc smiled. "Don't tell me you're not Danielle D'Oisseau," he said, grinning. "That Golden Globe was for *Tunnel of Rain*, the film your parents starred in and your dad directed."

"They're not my parents!" Riley said. "Honestly! I'm just a girl from Malibu who lives down the beach."

Marc shook his head back and forth, grinning the whole time. "You don't have to lie to me," he said. "I know what it's like being a famous person's kid. Once people find out, they try to use you and it ruins everything. Believe me, I've been there."

Riley tried to interrupt him, but Marc didn't want to hear it. He was so sure that she was Danielle D'Oisseau.

When she opened her mouth to argue, he put his index finger on her lips.

"Shhh," he said. "Don't worry. Your secret is safe with me. People like us have to stick together. That's why I never hang out with people who aren't connected to show business. They just don't understand."

What? Riley froze. She gulped, and her heart started beating hard.

He never hangs out with people who aren't connected to show business? Does that mean he'd dump me if I told him the truth?

For half a second, Riley was going to just blurt it all out anyway. How he had mistaken her for Danielle D'Oisseau when she was showing Jacques the way to the veterinarian.

But she couldn't do it. Not if it meant Marc would walk away.

They were having so much fun together! She didn't want it to end. And besides, maybe if he got to know her, then he'd start to like her for herself. She could always tell him the truth later…right?

"Yeah, you got me," Riley said with a shrug. "But don't tell anyone who I am, okay? I'm trying to keep a low profile."

"No problem." Marc nodded. "I'm all about keeping a low profile myself. So do you want to go out again?"

Huh? Is this date over? Riley wondered.

Then she realized that Mark thought he had dropped her off at home! He was ready to be on his way.

"Uh, sure!" Riley said.

"How about catching *Les Enfants Verts* at the Pepperdine campus Wednesday night? I saw a sign posted in town. It's open to the public, and it's supposed to be a really funny film," he said. "Unless you've already seen it."

It must be a French film, Riley thought. And judging from the way Marc said the title—with a perfect French accent—he probably speaks French really well.

"I haven't seen it yet," Riley said. "It sounds great."

"Excellent," Marc said. "They're showing it without subtitles, which will be awesome. I hate how the subtitles get in the way, don't you?"

No subtitles? Riley thought. Yikes!

She would have to sit through an entire French movie without understanding a word of it.

"Oh, great," Riley said, trying to sound enthusiastic instead of morose.

"So I'll meet you tomorrow night at seven," Marc said as he walked toward the deck steps.

"See you then," Riley called, still standing by Jacques's back door.

When Marc was gone, she headed back toward her own house.

What have I gotten myself into? she wondered.

She felt really guilty about lying. But what else could she do?

At least she had a plan—sort of. She'd tell him the truth eventually. When he knew her better. When he liked her for herself.

But for now there was only one choice.

She had to pretend to be French!

So Little Time
Mini Stereo System Sweepstakes

OFFICIAL RULES:

1. No purchase necessary.

2. To enter complete the official entry form or hand print your name, address, age, and phone number along with the words "*SO LITTLE TIME* Mini Stereo System Sweepstakes" on a 3" x 5" card and mail to: *SO LITTLE TIME* Mini Stereo System Sweepstakes, c/o HarperEntertainment, Attn: Children's Marketing Department, 10 East 53rd Street, New York, NY 10022. Entries must be received no later than August 31, 2003. Enter as often as you wish, but each entry must be mailed separately. One entry per envelope. Partially completed, illegible, or mechanically reproduced entries will not be accepted. Sponsors are not responsible for lost, late, mutilated, illegible, stolen, postage due, incomplete, or misdirected entries. All entries become the property of Dualstar Entertainment Group, LLC, and will not be returned.

3. Sweepstakes open to all legal residents of the United States (excluding Colorado and Rhode Island) who are between the ages of five and fifteen on August 31, 2003, excluding employees and immediate family members of HarperCollins Publishers, Inc., ("HarperCollins"), Parachute Properties and Parachute Press, Inc., and their respective subsidiaries and affiliates, officers, directors, shareholders, employees, agents, attorneys, and other representatives (individually and collectively "Parachute"), Dualstar Entertainment Group, LLC, and its subsidiaries and affiliates, officers, directors, shareholders, employees, agents, attorneys, and other representatives (individually and collectively "Dualstar"), and their respective parent companies, affiliates, subsidiaries, advertising, promotion and fulfillment agencies, and the persons with whom each of the above are domiciled. Offer void where prohibited or restricted by law.

4. Odds of winning depend on the total number of entries received. Approximately 200,000 sweepstakes announcements published. All prizes will be awarded. Winners will be randomly drawn on or about September 15, 2003, by HarperCollins, whose decisions are final. Potential winner will be notified by mail and will be required to sign and return an affidavit of eligibility and release of liability within 14 days of notification. Prizes won by minors will be awarded to parent or legal guardian who must sign and return all required legal documents. By acceptance of the prize, winner consents to the use of his or her name, photograph, likeness, and personal information by HarperCollins, Parachute, Dualstar, and for publicity purposes without further compensation except where prohibited.

5. a. One (1) Grand Prize Winner wins a Mini Stereo System. Approximate retail value is $250.00.
   b. Twenty-five (25) First Prize Winners win a Mary-Kate and Ashley music CD. Approximate retail value of each prize is $15.98.

6. Only one prize will be awarded per individual, family, or household. Prizes are non-transferable and cannot be sold or redeemed for cash. No cash substitute is available. Any federal, state, or local taxes are the responsibility of the winner. Sponsor may substitute prize of equal or greater retail value, if necessary, due to availability.

7. Additional terms: By participating, entrants agree a) to the official rules and decisions of the judges, which will be final in all respects; and to waive any claim to ambiguity of the official rules and b) to release, discharge, and hold harmless HarperCollins, Parachute, Dualstar, and their respective parent companies, affiliates, subsidiaries, advertising, promotion and fulfillment agencies from and against any and all liability or damages associated with acceptance, use, or misuse of any prize received in this Sweepstakes.

8. Any dispute arising from this Sweepstakes will be determined according to the laws of the State of New York, without reference to its conflict of law principles, and the entrants consent to the personal jurisdiction of the State and Federal courts located in New York County and agree that such courts have exclusive jurisdiction over all such disputes..

9. To obtain the name of the winners, please send your request and a self-addressed stamped envelope (residents of Vermont may omit return postage) to *SO LITTLE TIME* Mini Stereo System Sweepstakes Winners, c/o HarperEntertainment, Attn: Children's Marketing Department, 10 East 53rd Street, New York, NY 10022 by October 1, 2003. Sweepstakes Sponsor: HarperCollins Publishers, Inc.

Coming soon...A new
mary-kateandashley
2004 calendar!

Real **Calendars**
for **Real**
Girls

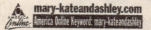

mary-kateandashley.com
America Online Keyword: mary-kateandashley

DUALSTAR
VIDEO

Own The Hit Series on DVD and Video!